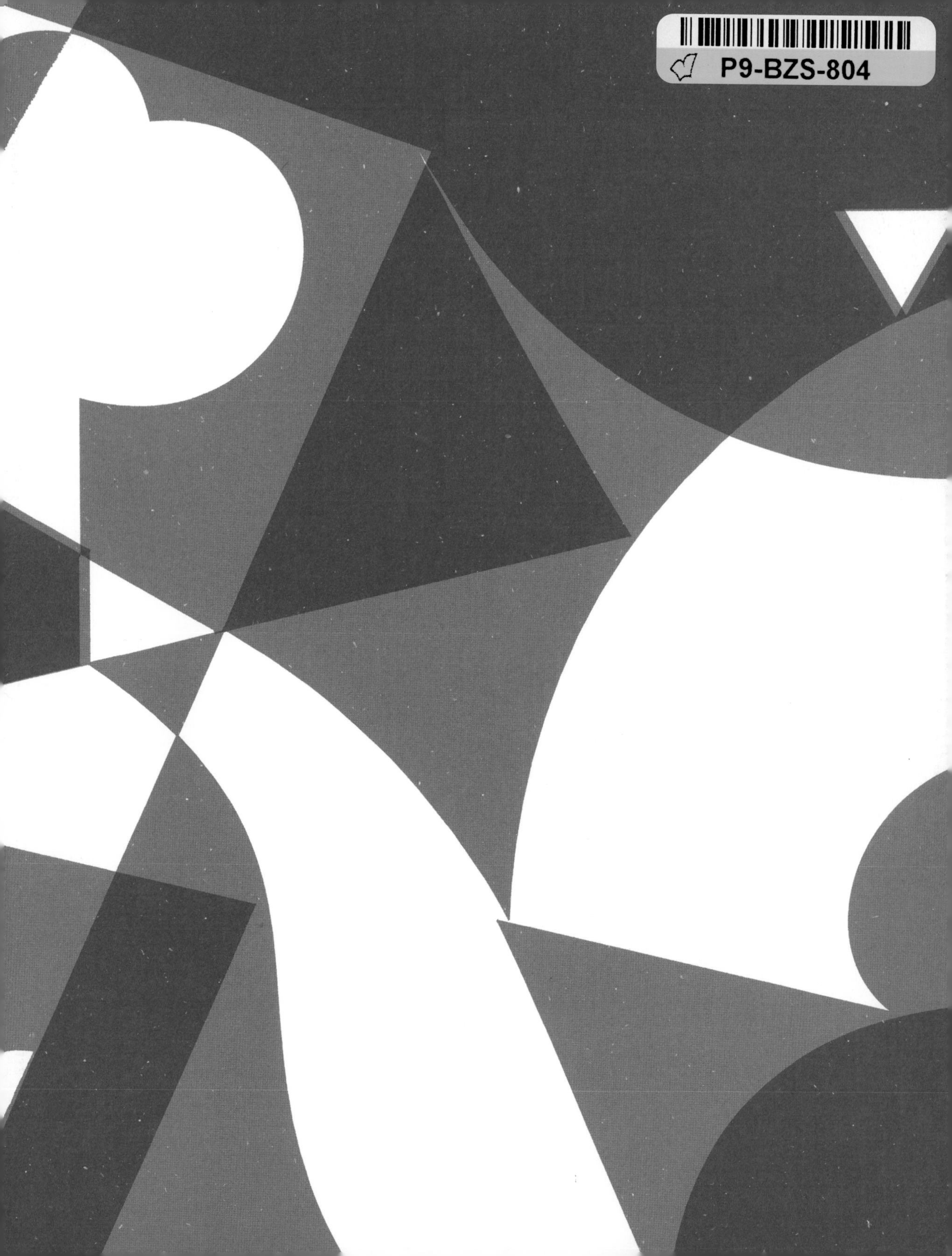

VANISHING ACT

FANTAGRAPHICS BOOKS INC.
7563 Lake City Way NE
Seattle, Washington, 98115

Editor and Associate Publisher: Eric Reynolds
Book Design: Roman Muradov and Keeli McCarthy
Production: Paul Baresh
Publisher: Gary Groth

Originally published by Dargaud as *Les desparitions*.
Translated from French by the author.

ISBN 978-1-68396-150-5
Library of Congress Control Number: 2018936477

First printing: December 2018
Printed in China

VANISHING ACT

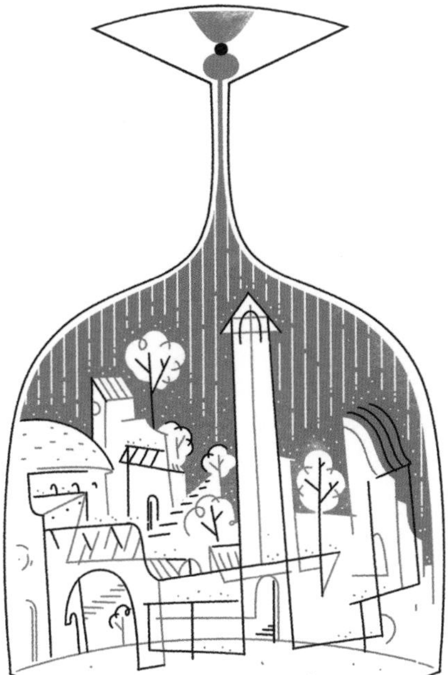

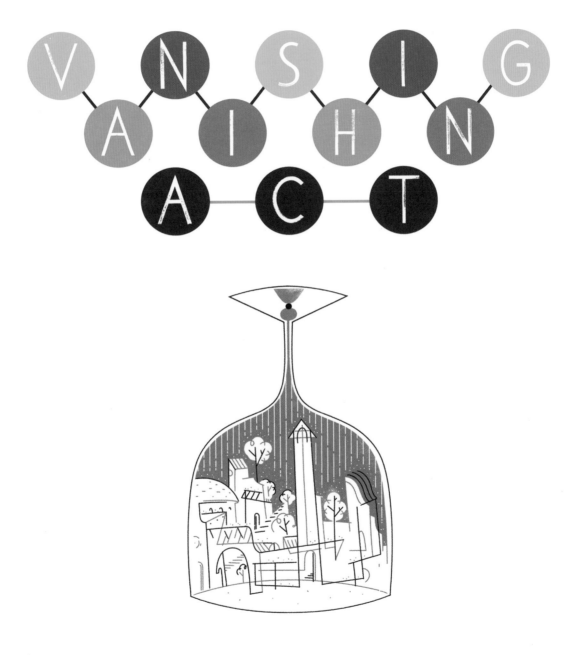

FANTAGRAPHICS BOOKS

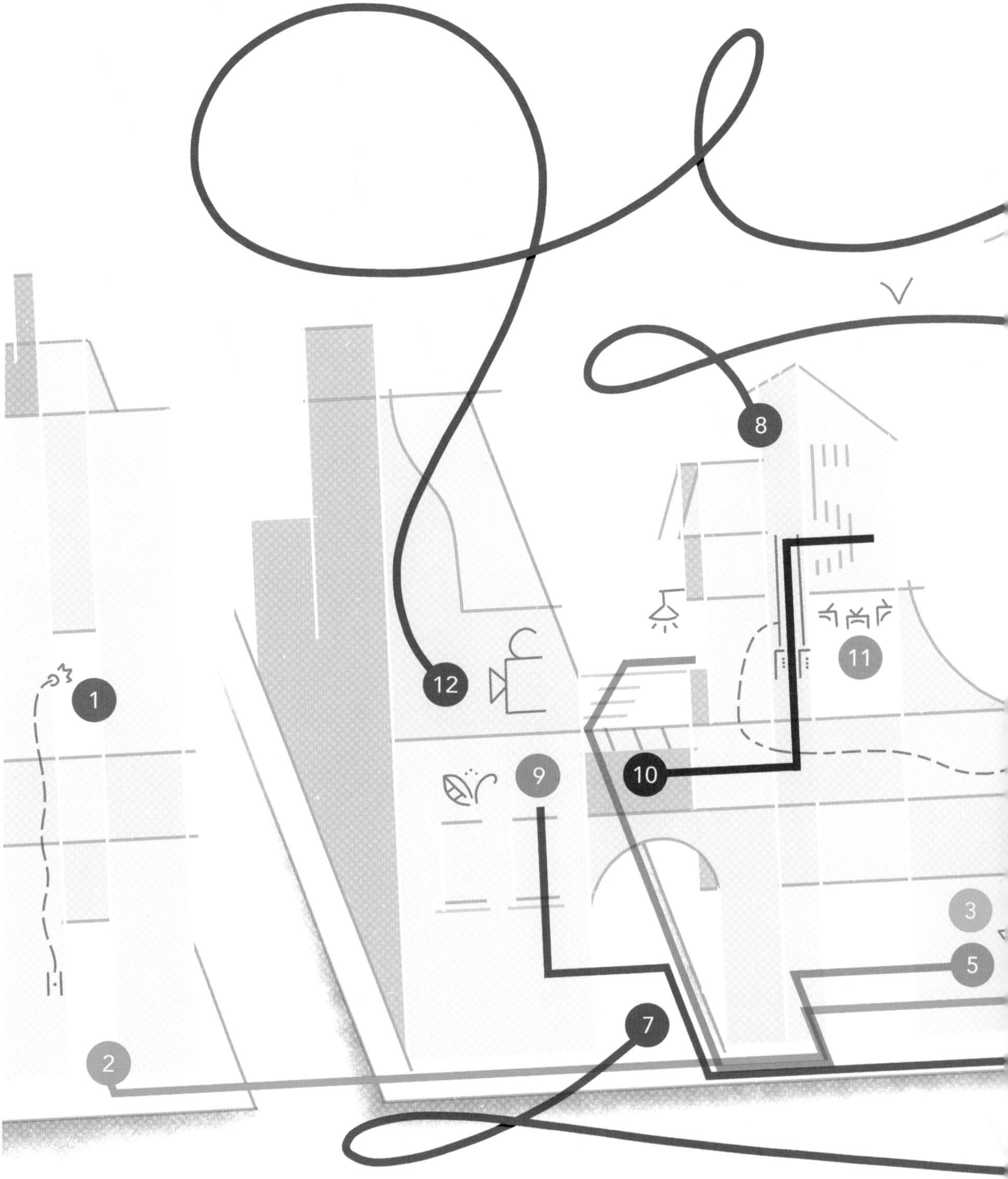

1
2
3
5
7
8
9
10
11
12

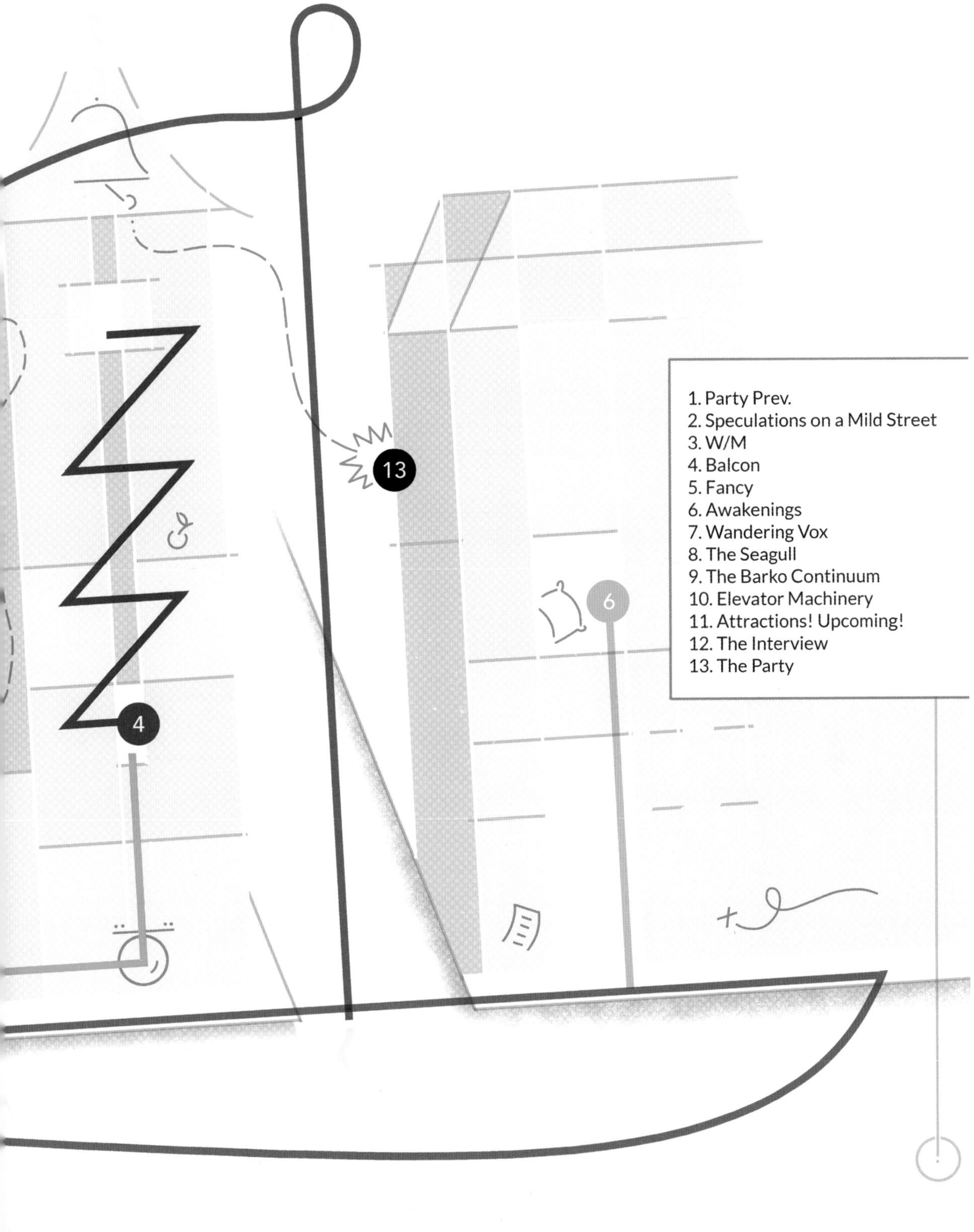
13
4
6
1. Party Prev.
2. Speculations on a Mild Street
3. W/M
4. Balcon
5. Fancy
6. Awakenings
7. Wandering Vox
8. The Seagull
9. The Barko Continuum
10. Elevator Machinery
11. Attractions! Upcoming!
12. The Interview
13. The Party

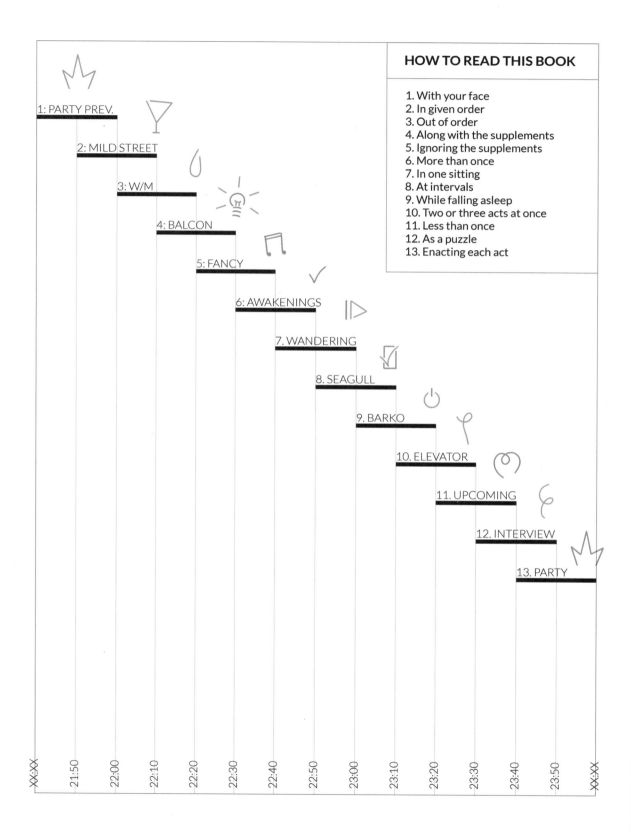

HOW TO READ THIS BOOK

1. With your face
2. In given order
3. Out of order
4. Along with the supplements
5. Ignoring the supplements
6. More than once
7. In one sitting
8. At intervals
9. While falling asleep
10. Two or three acts at once
11. Less than once
12. As a puzzle
13. Enacting each act

1: PARTY PREV.
2: MILD STREET
3: W/M
4: BALCON
5: FANCY
6: AWAKENINGS
7. WANDERING
8. SEAGULL
9. BARKO
10. ELEVATOR
11. UPCOMING
12. INTERVIEW
13. PARTY

XX:XX
21:50
22:00
22:10
22:20
22:30
22:40
22:50
23:00
23:10
23:20
23:30
23:40
23:50
XX:XX

Character	Description	Numbers	Portrait
Peter Hall	prolific actor of average renown	1, 11	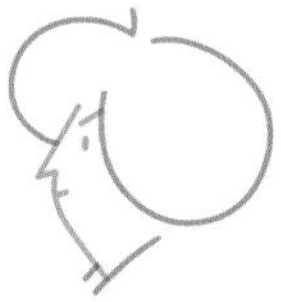
Val Fran R.	elm impersonator of moderate renown	11, 4, 9, 7	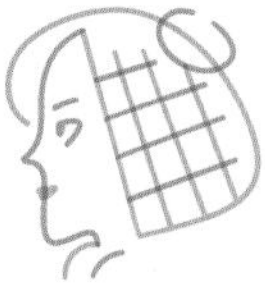
G. A.	comedic actor of diminishing renown	9, 1, 4, 2, 7, 11	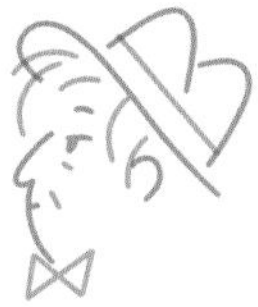
T. B.	production coordinator at Studio 5	9, 2, 12, 7, 4, 11	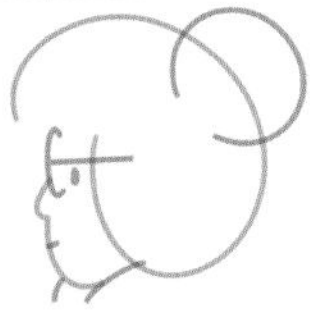
J. R.	freelance journalist	3, 5	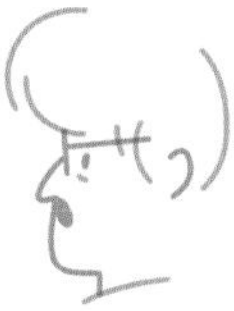
R. R.	aspiring journalist, J. R.'s fiancé	5, 3	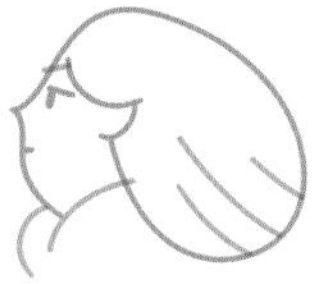
Slats Blatteroid	art critic of some renown	11, 5	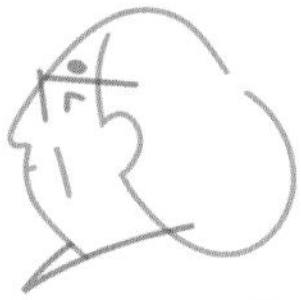
Carrie Blatteroid	senior lecturer, Slats Blatteroid's wife	5	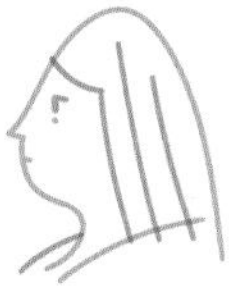
Simon B.	camera operator at Studio 5	10, 8, 7, 9, 6	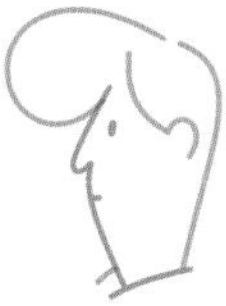
Robert B.	poet of nominal renown, Simon B.'s uncle	11, 8	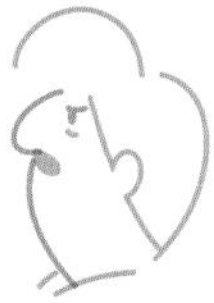
Gerald Bland	producer at Studio 5	10, 7, 8, 9	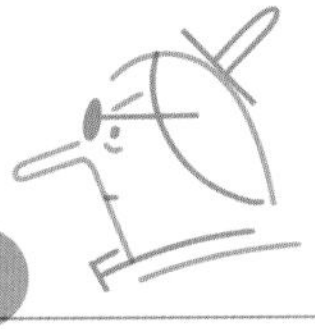
Madeleine F.	make-up artist at Studio 5, actor of minimal renown	11, 7, 9	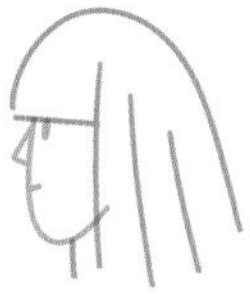
Belinda C.	freelance writer of mild renown	7, 9	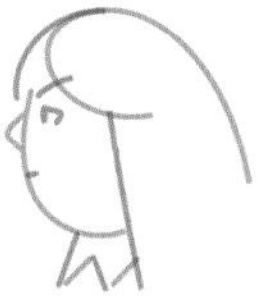
F. Premise	bookstore owner of no renown	7	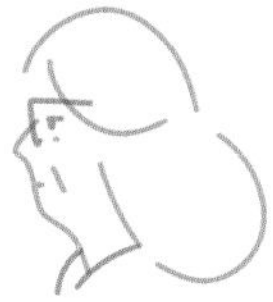
Barko	Belinda's dog of eternal renown	9	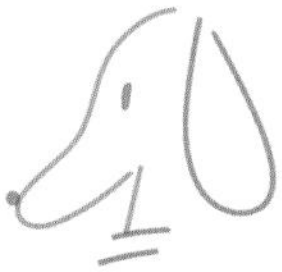
Bailey and Braxton	the cats of Slats and Carrie Blatteroid	5	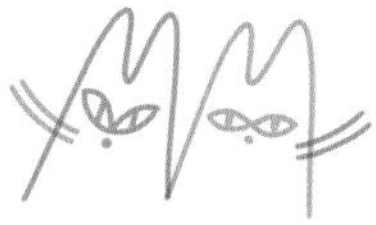
Sybil Same	veteran actor of considerable renown	11, 13	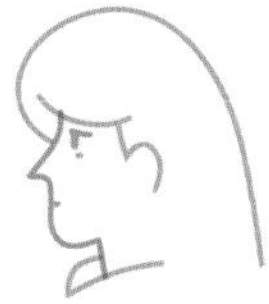
M. Fallotin	author and artist of immeasurable renown	11, 7, 12, 9	

ACT 1
Party Prev.

CAST
Peter Hall
G. A.

SCENE
Peter Hall's apartment
Peter Hall's daydream

TIME
XX:XX-22:00

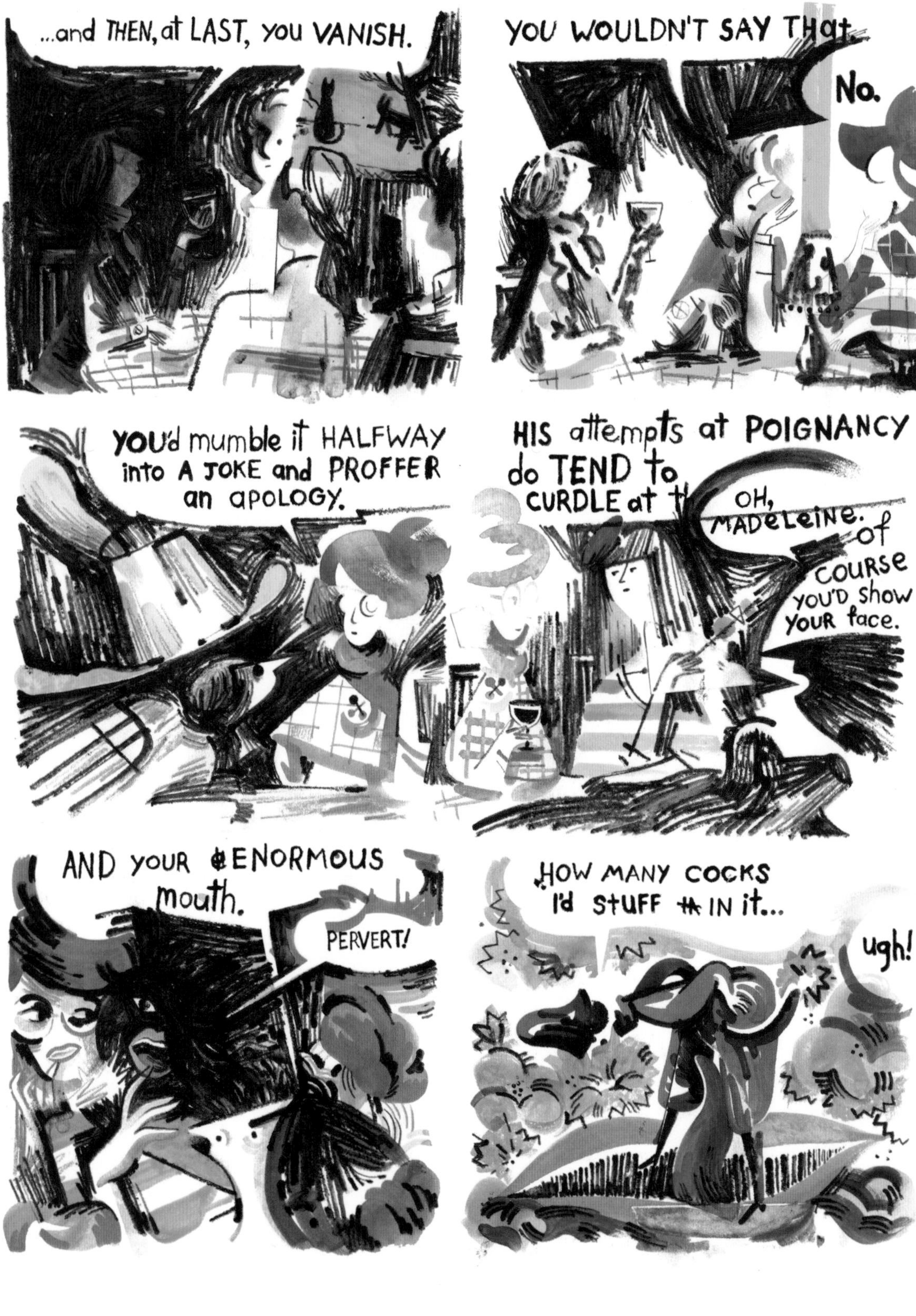

...and THEN, at LAST, you VANISH.
YOU WOULDN'T SAY That
No.
YOU'd mumble it HALFWAY into A JOKE and PROFFER an apology.
HIS attempts at POIGNANCY do TEND to CURDLE at t
OH, MADELEINE.
of COURSE YOU'D show YOUR face.
AND YOUR ENORMOUS mouth.
PERVERT!
HOW MANY COCKS I'd STUFF IN it...
ugh!

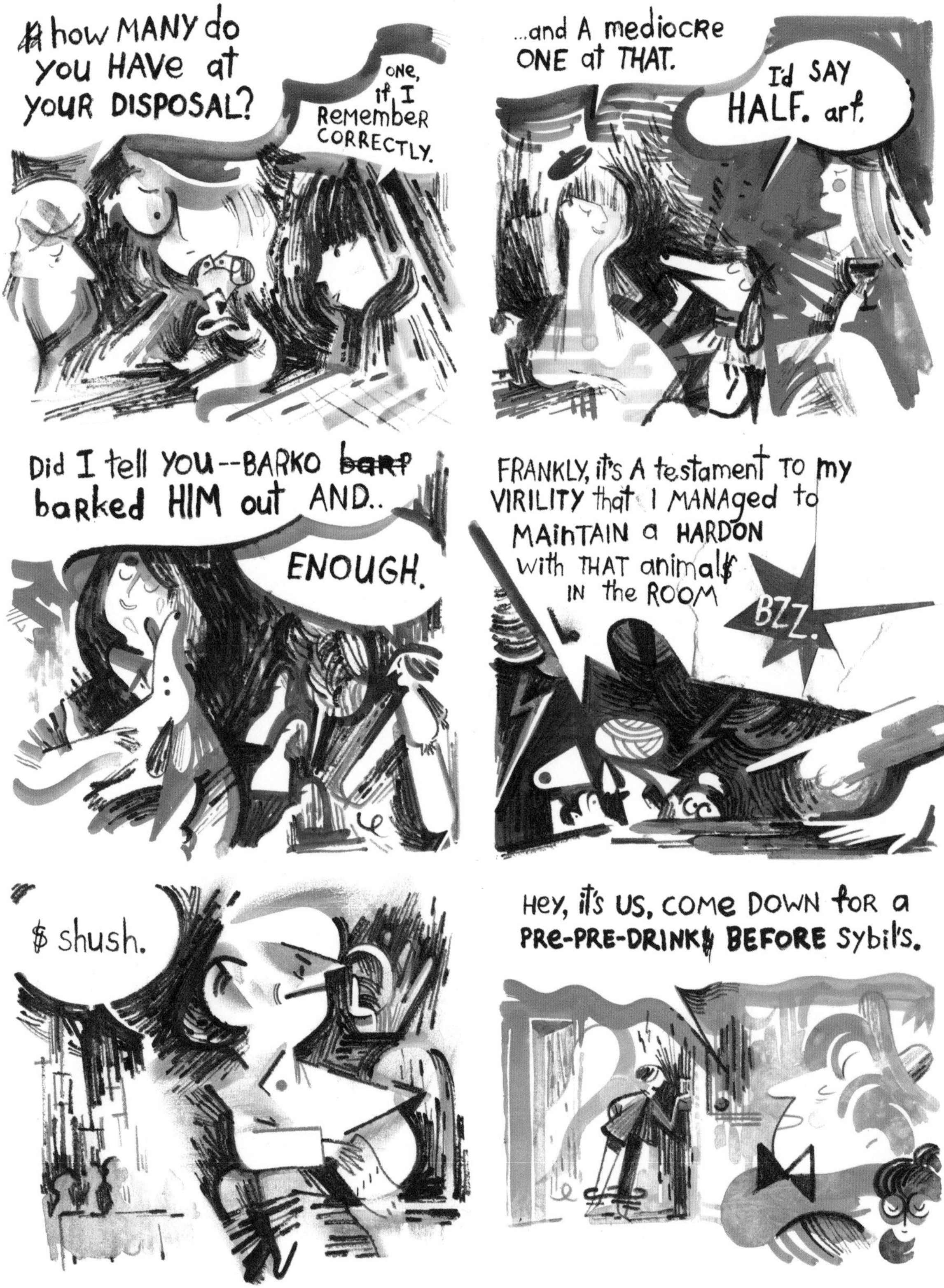
A how MANY do you HAVE at your DISPOSAL?
ONE, if I Remember CORRECTLY.
...and A mediocre ONE at THAT.
I'd SAY HALF. arf.
Did I tell YOU--BARKO barp barked HIM out AND..
ENOUGH.
FRANKLY, it's A testament TO my VIRILITY that I MANAGED to MAINTAIN a HARDON with THAT animal$ IN the ROOM
BZZ.
$ shush.
Hey, it's US, COME DOWN for a PRE-PRE-DRINK$ BEFORE Sybil's.

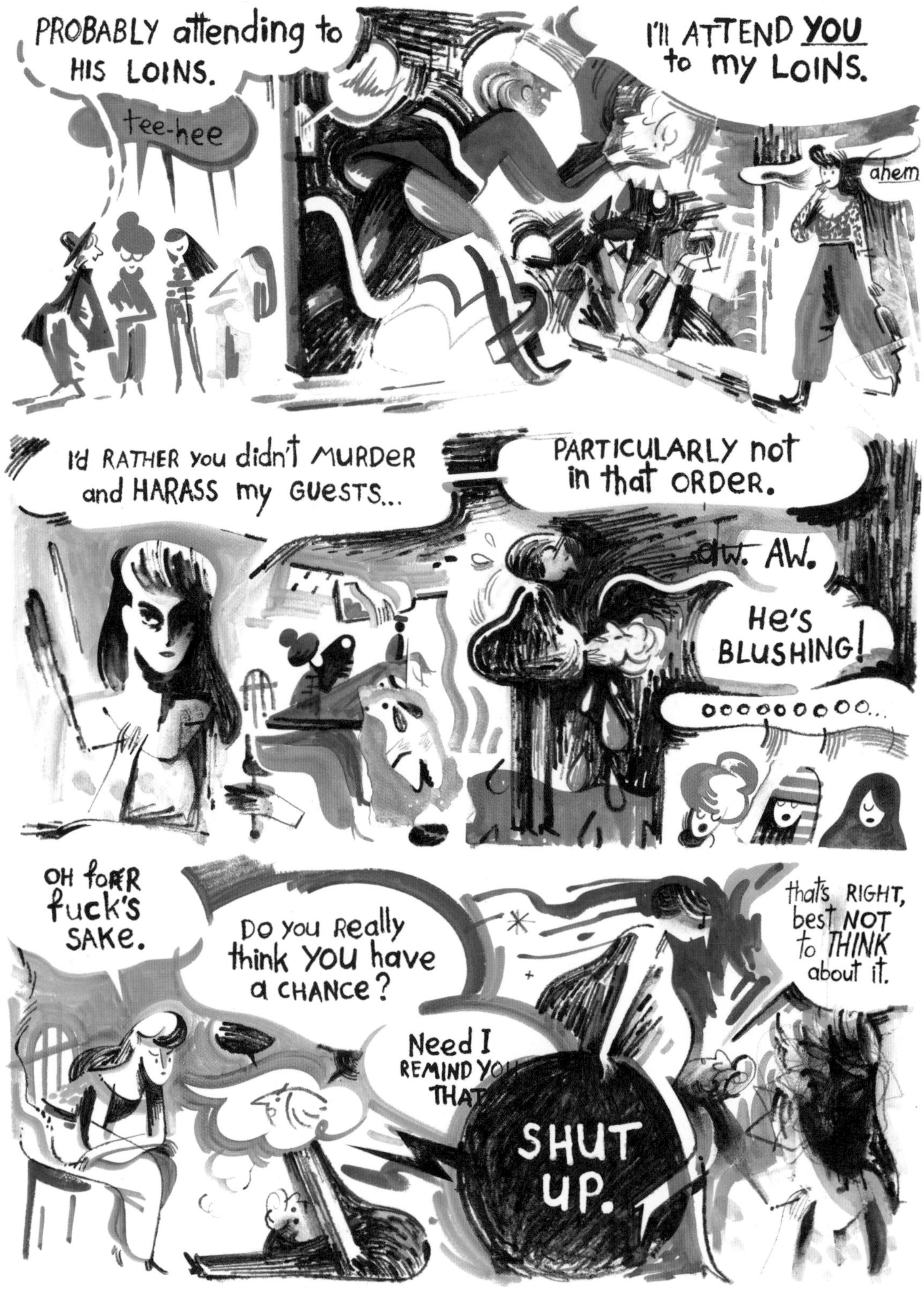
PROBABLY attending to HIS LOINS.
tee-hee
I'll ATTEND YOU to my LOINS.
ahem
I'd RATHER you didn't MURDER and HARASS my GUESTS...
PARTICULARLY not in that ORDER.
AW. AW.
He's BLUSHING!
oooooooooo...
OH forRR fuck's SAKE.
Do you Really think YOU have a CHANCE?
Need I REMIND YOU THAT
SHUT UP.
that's RIGHT, best NOT to THINK about it.

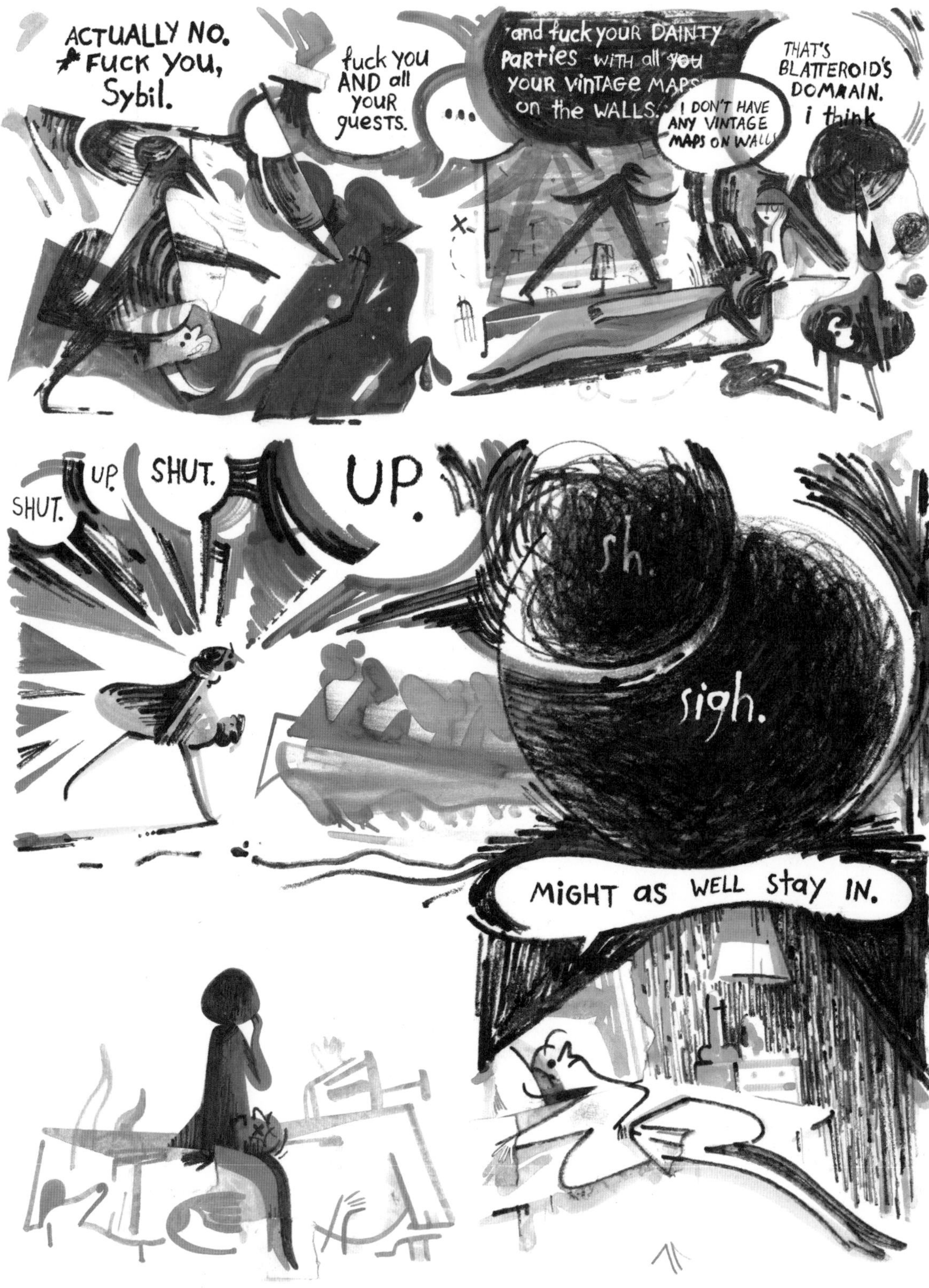
ACTUALLY NO. FUCK YOU, Sybil.
fuck YOU AND all YOUR guests.
...
and fuck YOUR DAINTY parties with all you YOUR VINTAGE MAPS on the WALLS.
I DON'T HAVE ANY VINTAGE MAPS ON WALLS
THAT'S BLATTEROID'S DOMAAIN. i think
SHUT.
UP.
SHUT.
UP.
sh.
sigh.
MIGHT as WELL stay IN.

ACT 2
Speculations on a Mild Street

CAST
G. A.
T. B.

SCENE
Outside Peter Hall's apartment
Mild Street
Studio 5 Bar
the Adjoining Laundromat

TIME
21:50-22:10

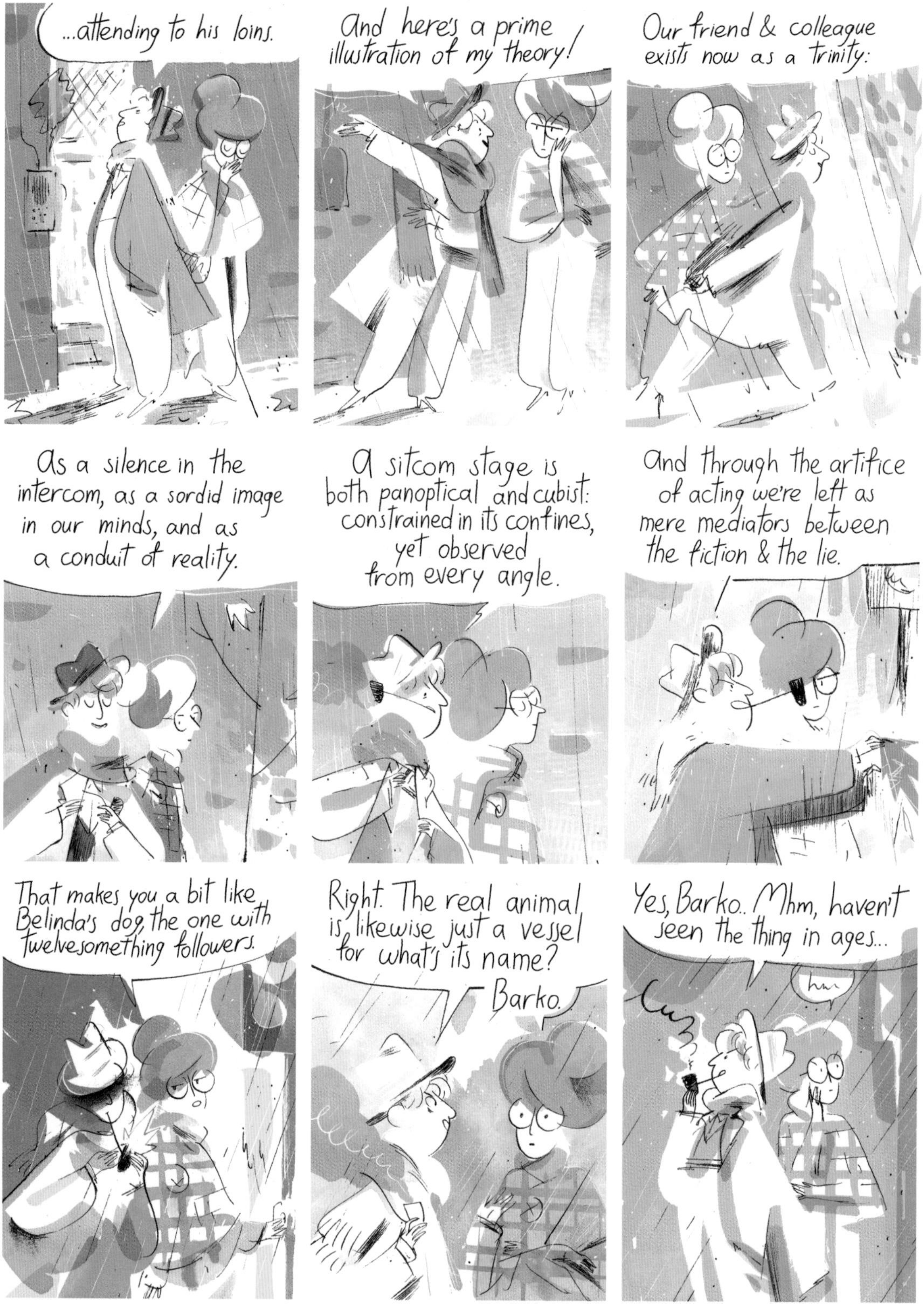
...attending to his loins.
And here's a prime illustration of my theory!
Our friend & colleague exists now as a trinity:
As a silence in the intercom, as a sordid image in our minds, and as a conduit of reality.
A sitcom stage is both panoptical and cubist: constrained in its confines, yet observed from every angle.
And through the artifice of acting we're left as mere mediators between the fiction & the lie.
That makes you a bit like Belinda's dog, the one with twelvesomething followers.
Right. The real animal is likewise just a vessel for what's its name?
Barko.
Yes, Barko.. Mhm, haven't seen the thing in ages...

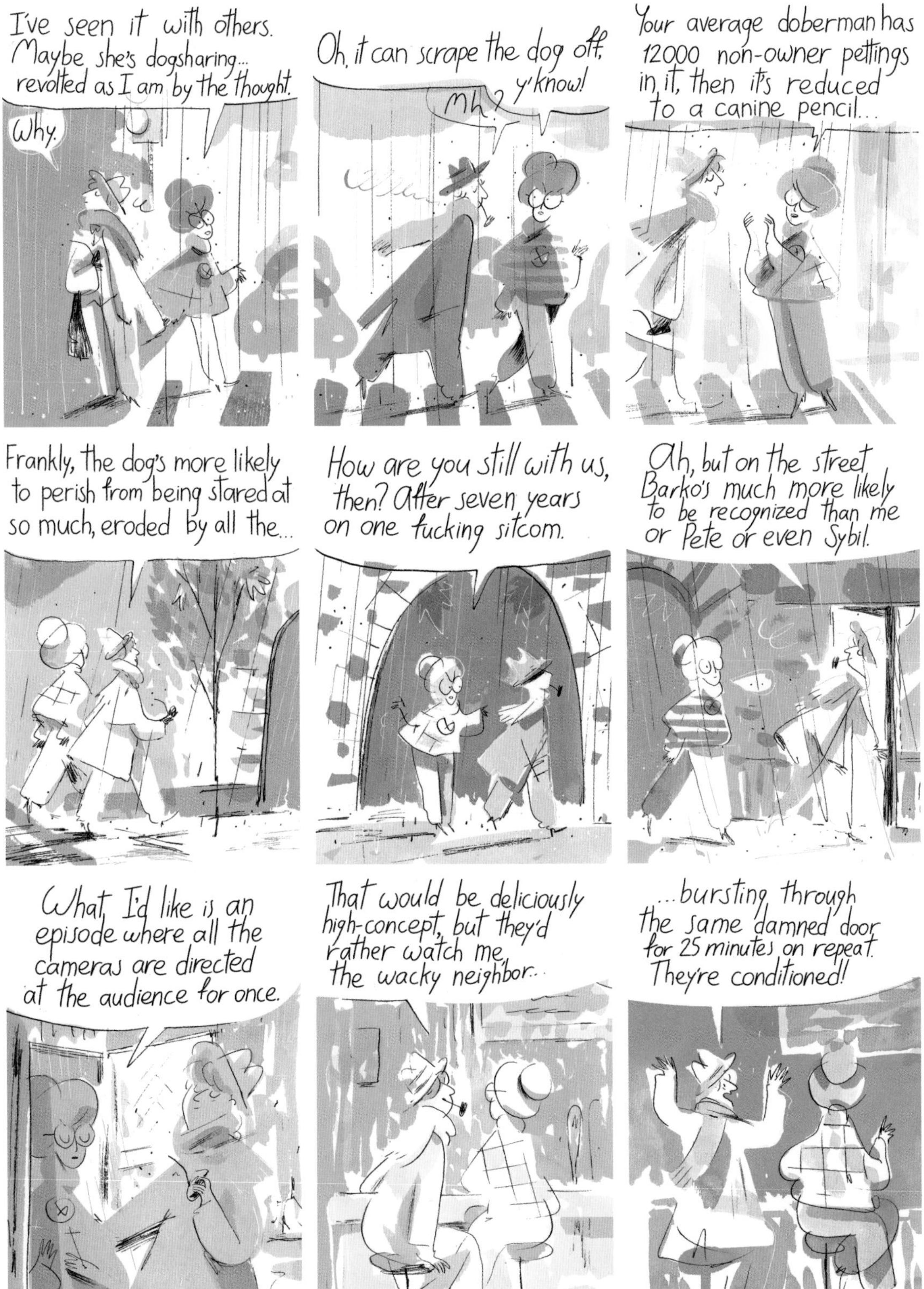
I've seen it with others. Maybe she's dogsharing... revolted as I am by the thought.
Why.
Oh, it can scrape the dog off, y'know!
Mh?
Your average doberman has 12000 non-owner pettings in it, then it's reduced to a canine pencil...
Frankly, the dog's more likely to perish from being stared at so much, eroded by all the...
How are you still with us, then? After seven years on one fucking sitcom.
Ah, but on the street Barko's much more likely to be recognized than me or Pete or even Sybil.
What I'd like is an episode where all the cameras are directed at the audience for once.
That would be deliciously high-concept, but they'd rather watch me, the wacky neighbor..
...bursting through the same damned door for 25 minutes on repeat. They're conditioned!

An average episode yields one or two catchphrases to be later recycled during a lull in the script.

These are little rewards for the obedient viewer who tunes in weekly...

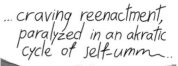
... craving reenactment, paralyzed in an akratic cycle of self-umm...

Well, that's <u>quite</u> a bit far-fetched, but ok, the reception of the first episode was abysmal.

Exactly! And the ratings rose in a geometric progression following not an increase in quality...

no.

...but a steady accumulation of catchphrases!

My point is, if it goes on indefinitely, one day there will be an entire episode...

...of Jarry in the House of Rue that contains <u>no</u> story at all,...

...just a succession of references to previous episodes!

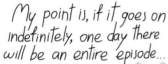

To the uninitiated it may sound like an abstract poem.

To a devotee it would make all other sensory experience redundant.

Each line recited out of context, without fault, exactly as expected, and endlessly, whatevermore!

ok...

So this pencil was a doberman once?..

More likely a pomeranian.

And this whole enter-through--a-washing-machine-thing is that a metaphor

Yep.

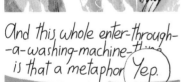

Well, this is a new low.

ACT 3
W/M

CAST
J. R.
R. R.

SCENE
Studio 5 Bar

TIME
22:00-22:20

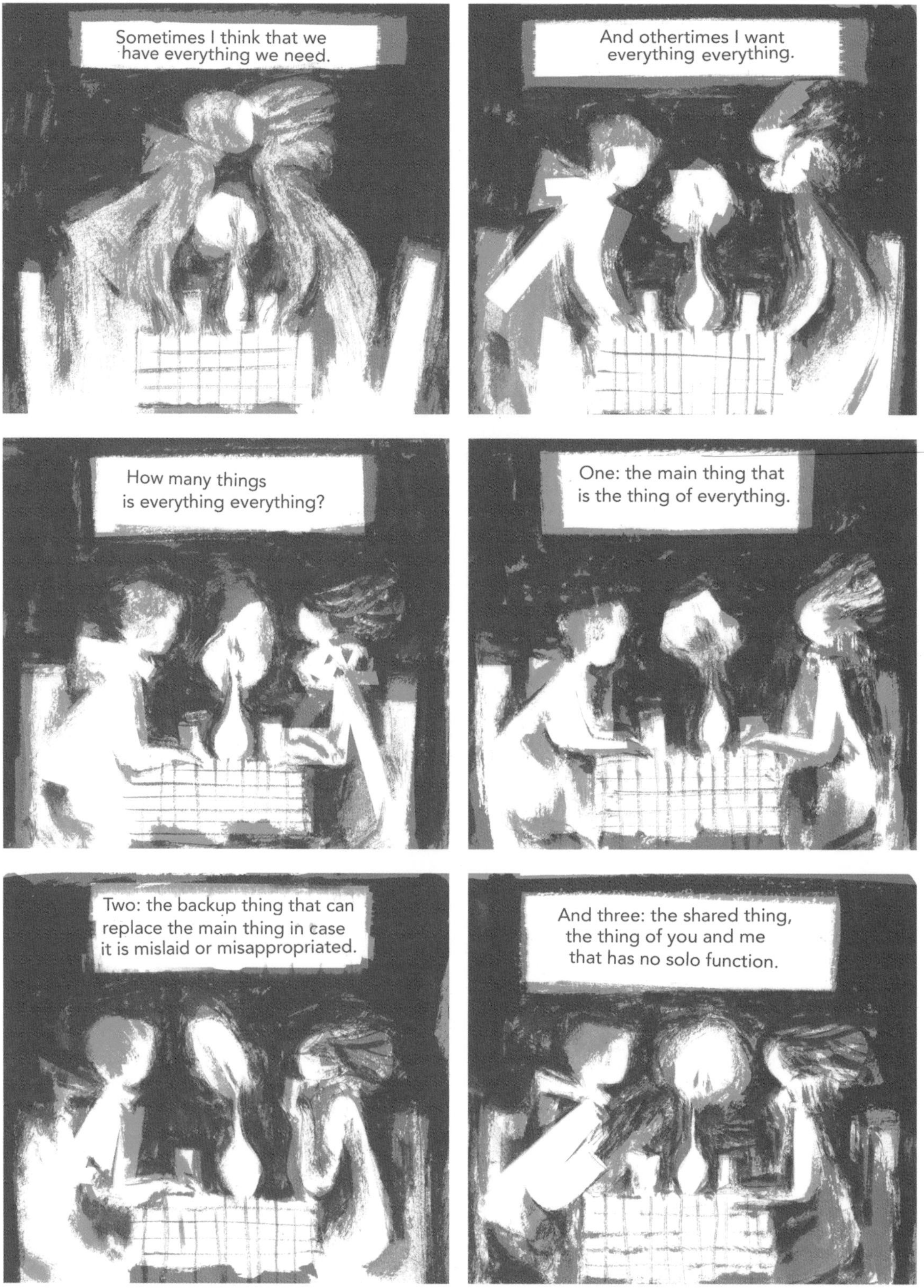
Sometimes I think that we have everything we need.
And othertimes I want everything everything.
How many things is everything everything?
One: the main thing that is the thing of everything.
Two: the backup thing that can replace the main thing in case it is mislaid or misappropriated.
And three: the shared thing, the thing of you and me that has no solo function.

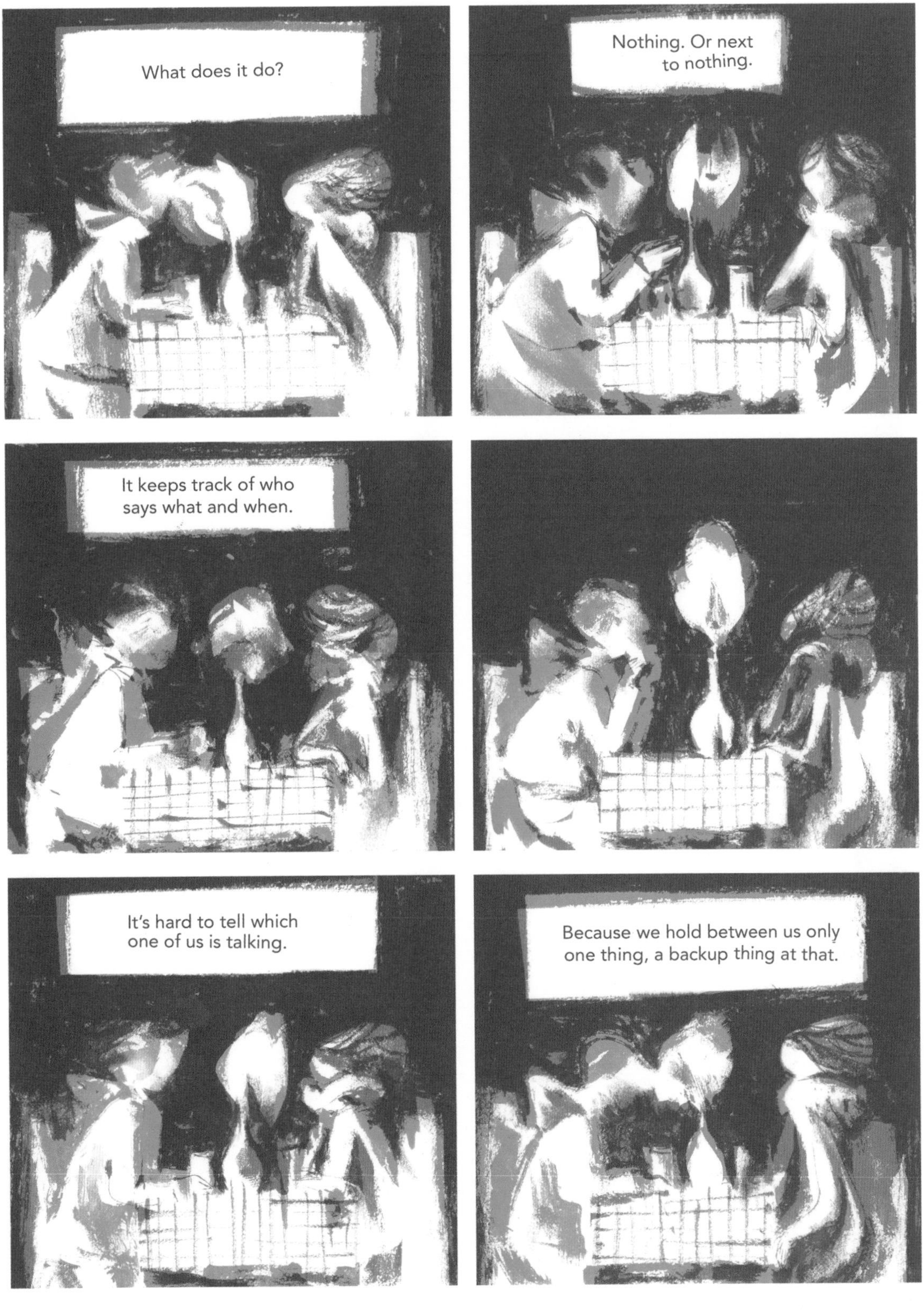
What does it do?
Nothing. Or next to nothing.
It keeps track of who says what and when.
It's hard to tell which one of us is talking.
Because we hold between us only one thing, a backup thing at that.

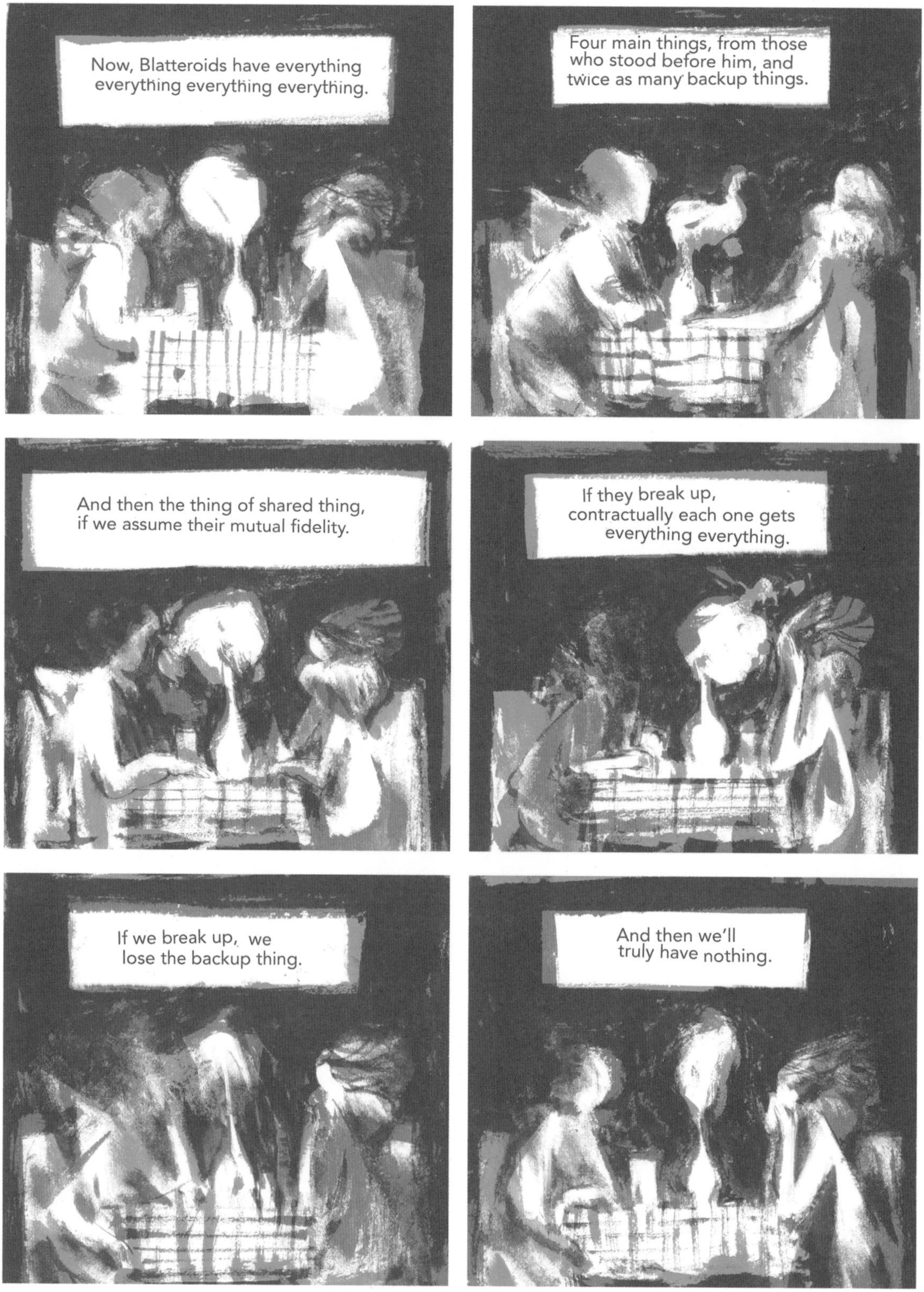
Now, Blatteroids have everything everything everything everything.
Four main things, from those who stood before him, and twice as many backup things.
And then the thing of shared thing, if we assume their mutual fidelity.
If they break up, contractually each one gets everything everything.
If we break up, we lose the backup thing.
And then we'll truly have nothing.

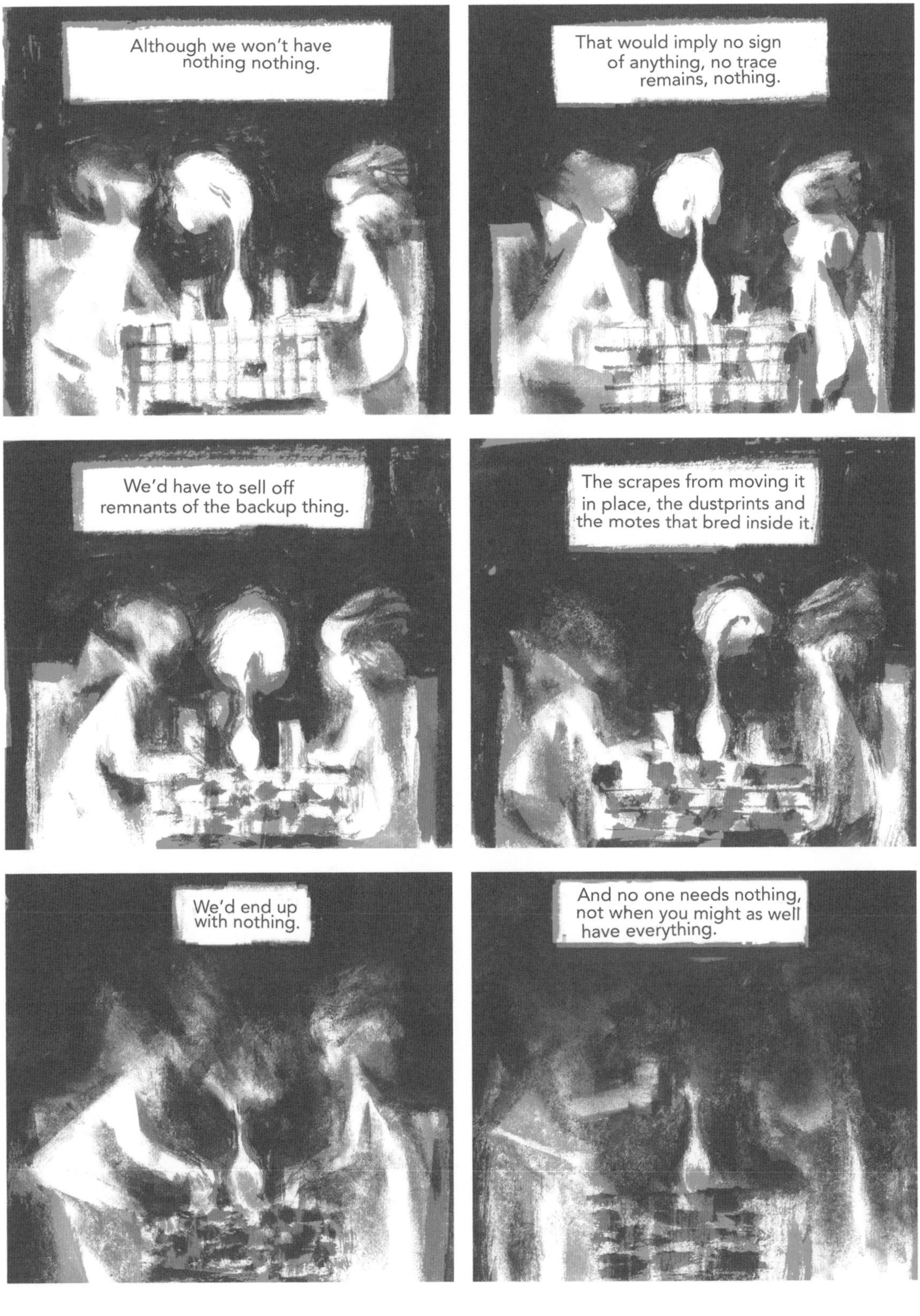
Although we won't have nothing nothing.
That would imply no sign of anything, no trace remains, nothing.
We'd have to sell off remnants of the backup thing.
The scrapes from moving it in place, the dustprints and the motes that bred inside it.
We'd end up with nothing.
And no one needs nothing, not when you might as well have everything.

ACT 4
Balcon

CAST
G. A.
T. B.
Val Fran R.

SCENE
Club Balcon

TIME
22:10-22:30

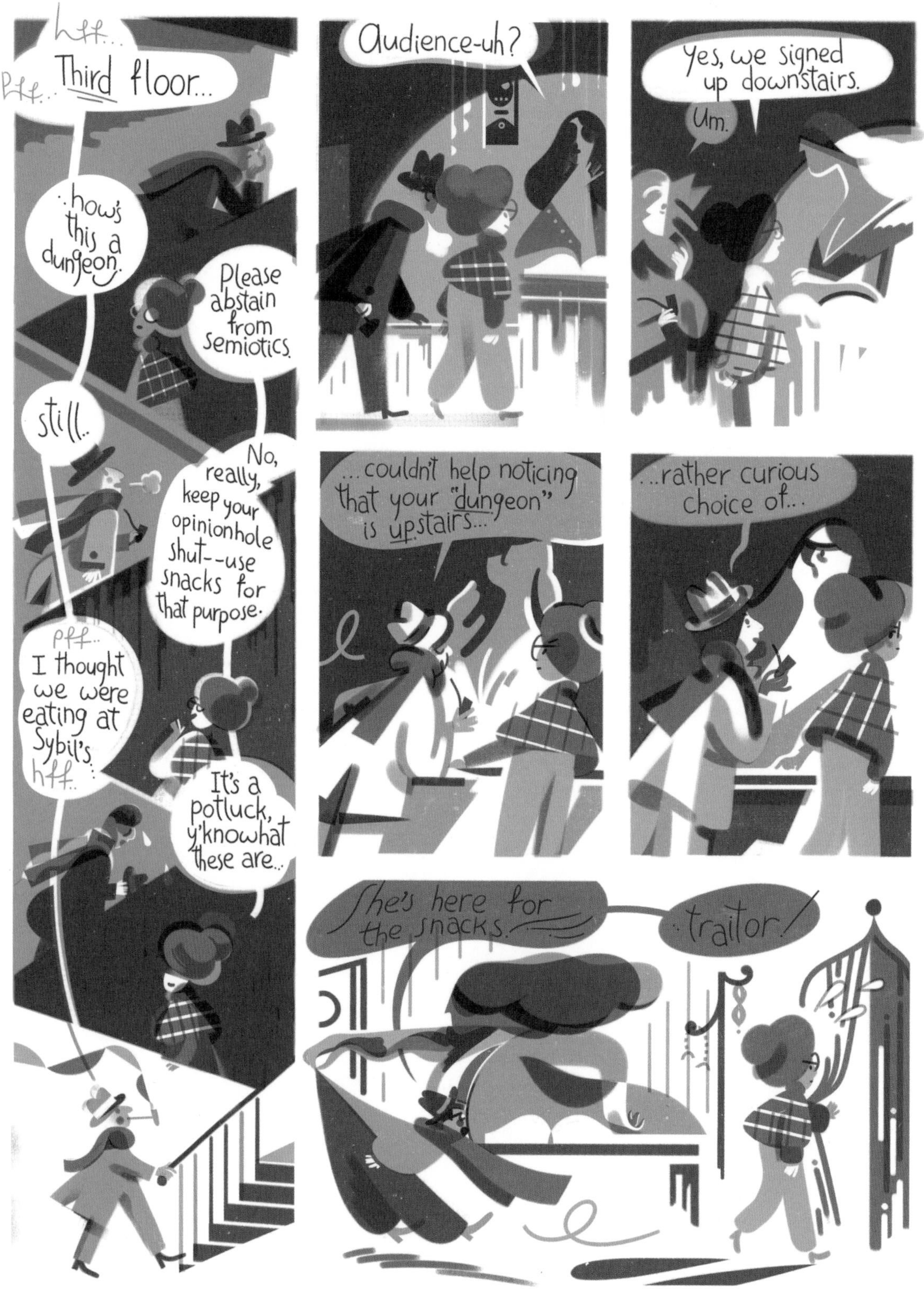
hff...
Pff... Third floor...
..how's this a dungeon.
Please abstain from semiotics.
still..
No, really, keep your opinionhole shut--use snacks for that purpose.
pff..
I thought we were eating at Sybil's..
hff..
It's a potluck, y'knowhat these are...
Audience-uh?
Yes, we signed up downstairs.
Um.
...couldn't help noticing that your "dungeon" is upstairs...
...rather curious choice of...
She's here for the snacks.
..traitor!

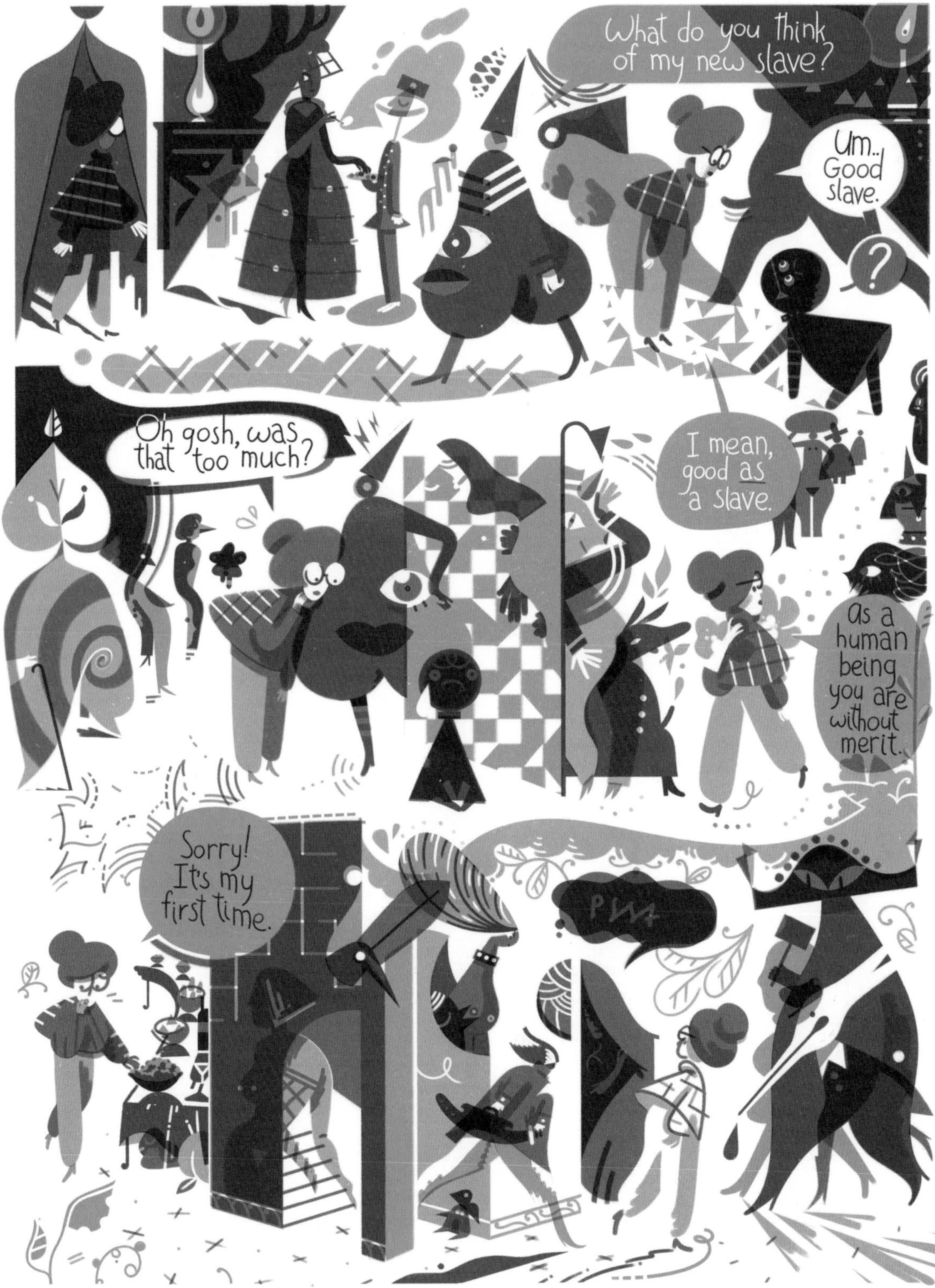
What do you think of my new slave?
Um.. Good slave.
?
Oh gosh, was that too much?
I mean, good as a slave.
As a human being you are without merit.
Sorry! It's my first time.

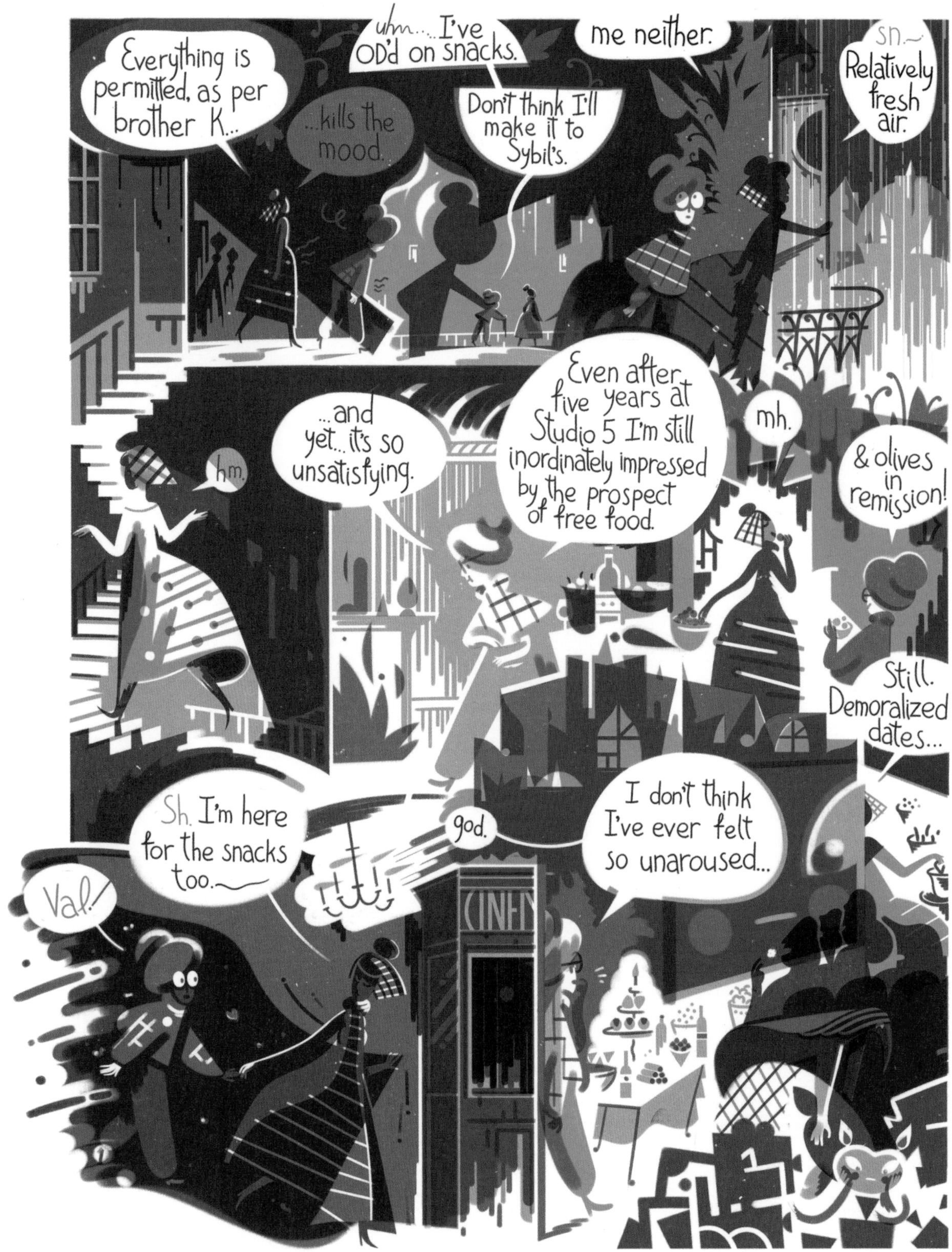
Everything is permitted, as per brother K...
...kills the mood.
uhm.... I've OD'd on snacks.
Don't think I'll make it to Sybil's.
me neither.
sn.~ Relatively fresh air.
hm.
...and yet... it's so unsatisfying.
Even after five years at Studio 5 I'm still inordinately impressed by the prospect of free food.
mh.
& olives in remission!
Still. Demoralized dates...
Sh. I'm here for the snacks too.~
god.
I don't think I've ever felt so unaroused...
Val!
CINE

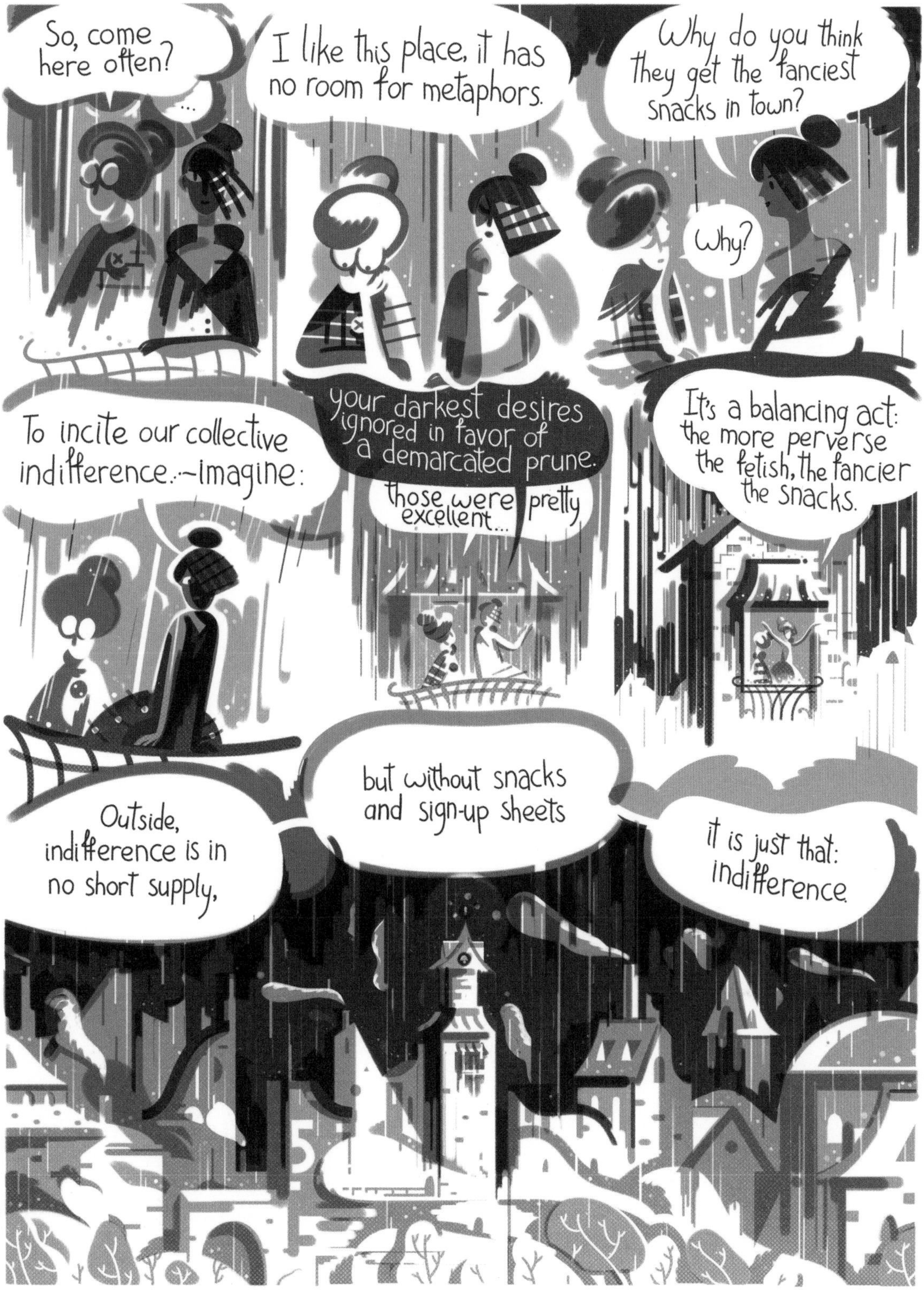
So, come here often?
...
I like this place, it has no room for metaphors.
Why do you think they get the fanciest snacks in town?
Why?
To incite our collective indifference...—imagine:
your darkest desires ignored in favor of a demarcated prune.
those were pretty excellent...
It's a balancing act: the more perverse the fetish, the fancier the snacks.
Outside, indifference is in no short supply,
but without snacks and sign-up sheets
it is just that: indifference.

ACT 5
Fancy

CAST
J. R.
R. R.
Slats Blatteroid
Carrie Blatteroid
Bailey and Braxton

SCENE
Mild Street
the Blatteroids' apartments

TIME
22:20-22:40

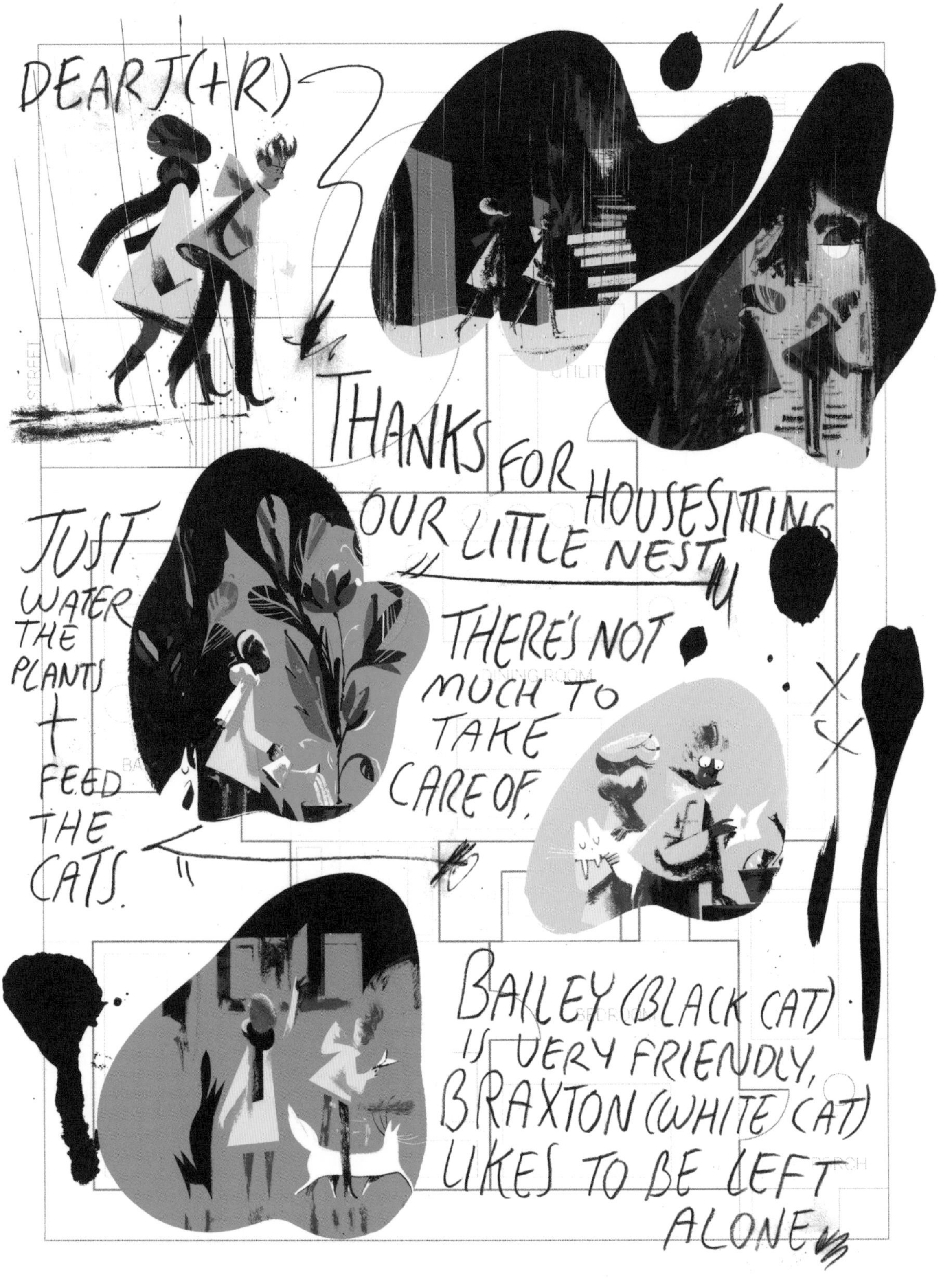
DEAR J (+R)
THANKS FOR HOUSESITTING OUR LITTLE NEST
JUST WATER THE PLANTS + FEED THE CATS.
THERE'S NOT MUCH TO TAKE CARE OF.
BAILEY (BLACK CAT) IS VERY FRIENDLY, BRAXTON (WHITE CAT) LIKES TO BE LEFT ALONE

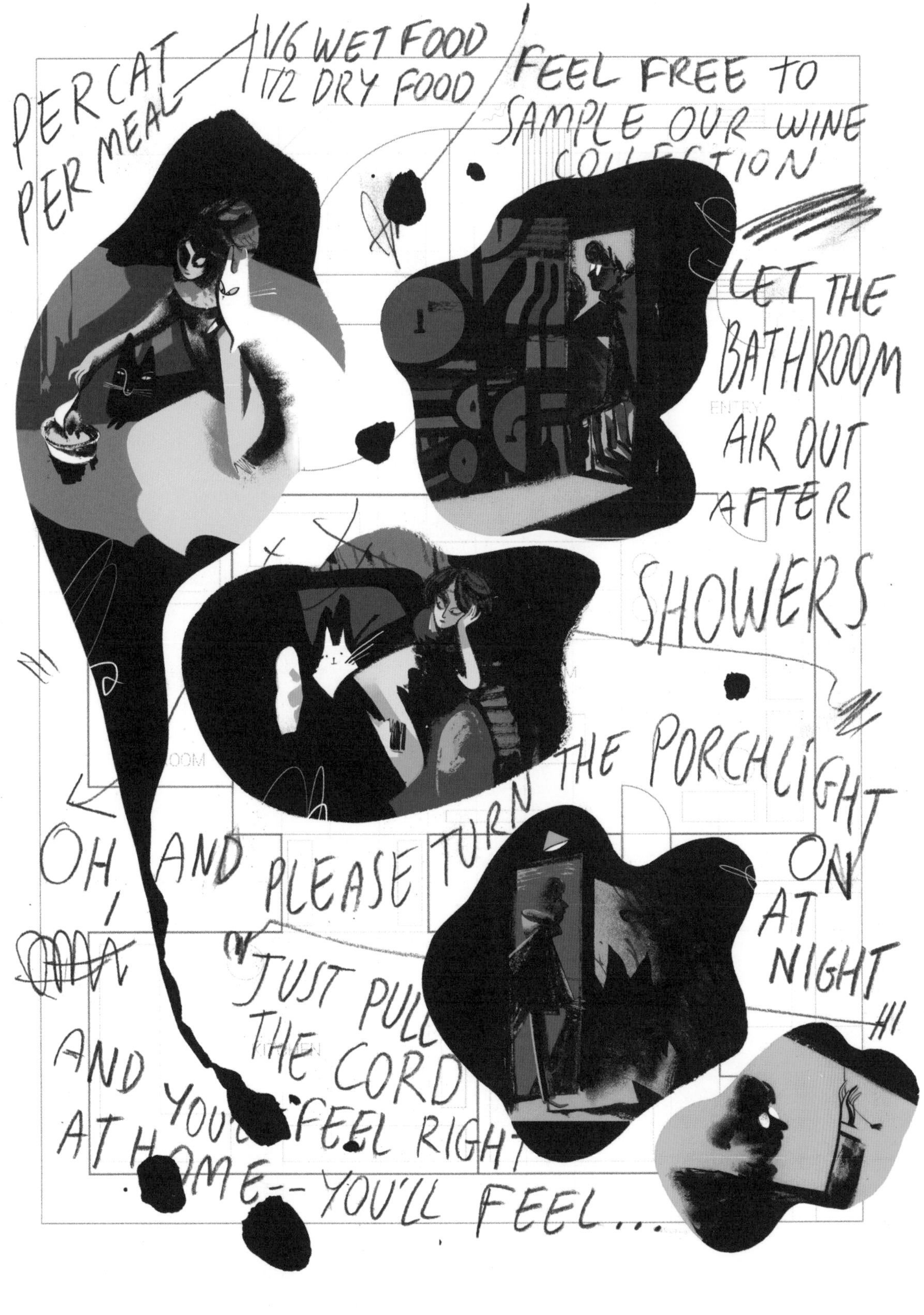
PER CAT PER MEAL
1/6 WET FOOD
1/2 DRY FOOD
FEEL FREE TO SAMPLE OUR WINE COLLECTION
LET THE BATHROOM AIR OUT AFTER SHOWERS
OH, AND PLEASE TURN THE PORCHLIGHT ON AT NIGHT
JUST PULL THE CORD
HI
AND YOU'LL FEEL RIGHT AT HOME-- YOU'LL FEEL...

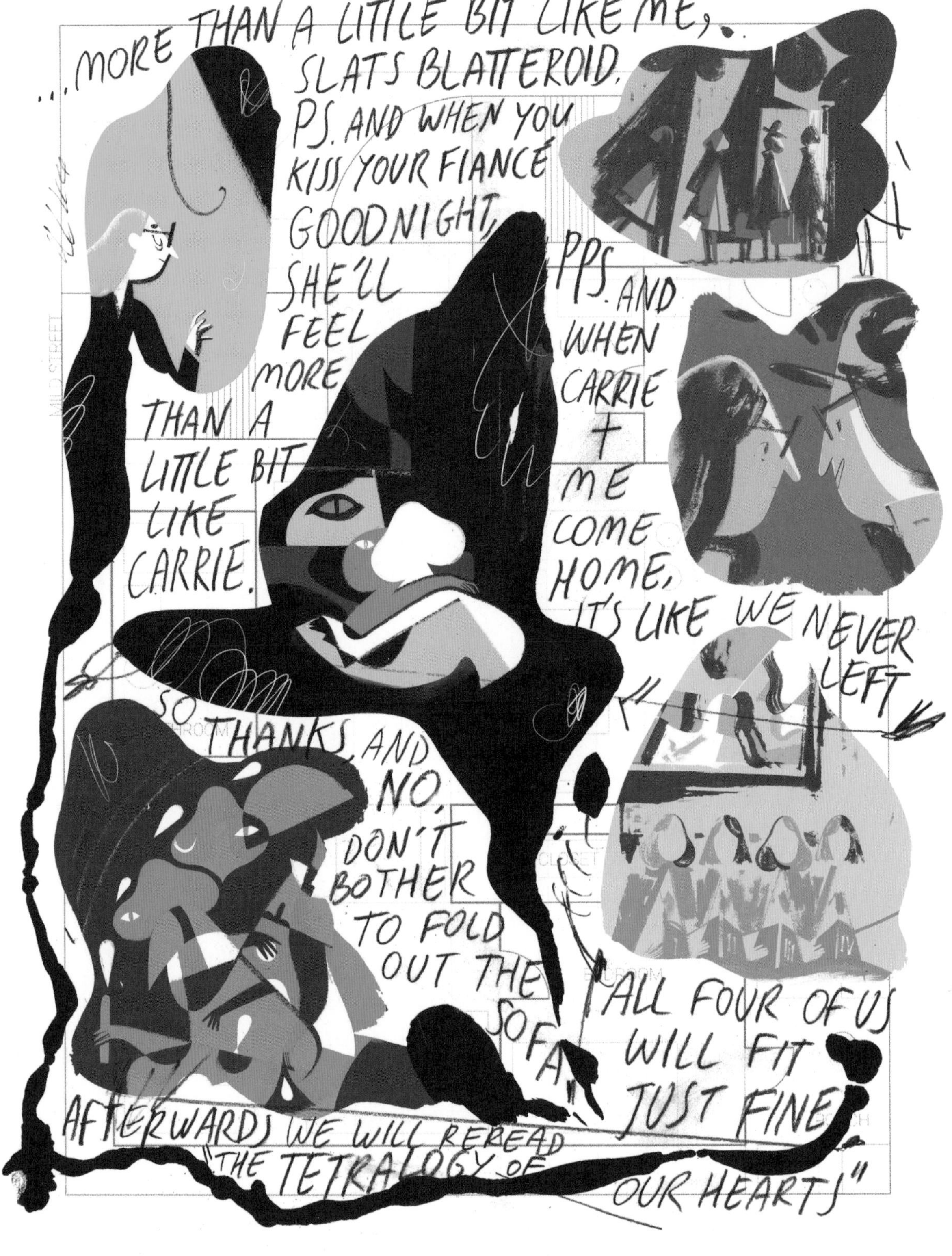

...MORE THAN A LITTLE BIT LIKE ME,..
SLATS BLATTEROID,
P.S. AND WHEN YOU KISS YOUR FIANCÉ GOODNIGHT, SHE'LL FEEL MORE THAN A LITTLE BIT LIKE CARRIE.
P.P.S. AND WHEN CARRIE + ME COME HOME, IT'S LIKE WE NEVER LEFT
SO THANKS, AND NO, DON'T BOTHER TO FOLD OUT THE SOFA.
ALL FOUR OF US WILL FIT JUST FINE.
AFTERWARDS WE WILL REREAD "THE TETRALOGY OF OUR HEARTS"

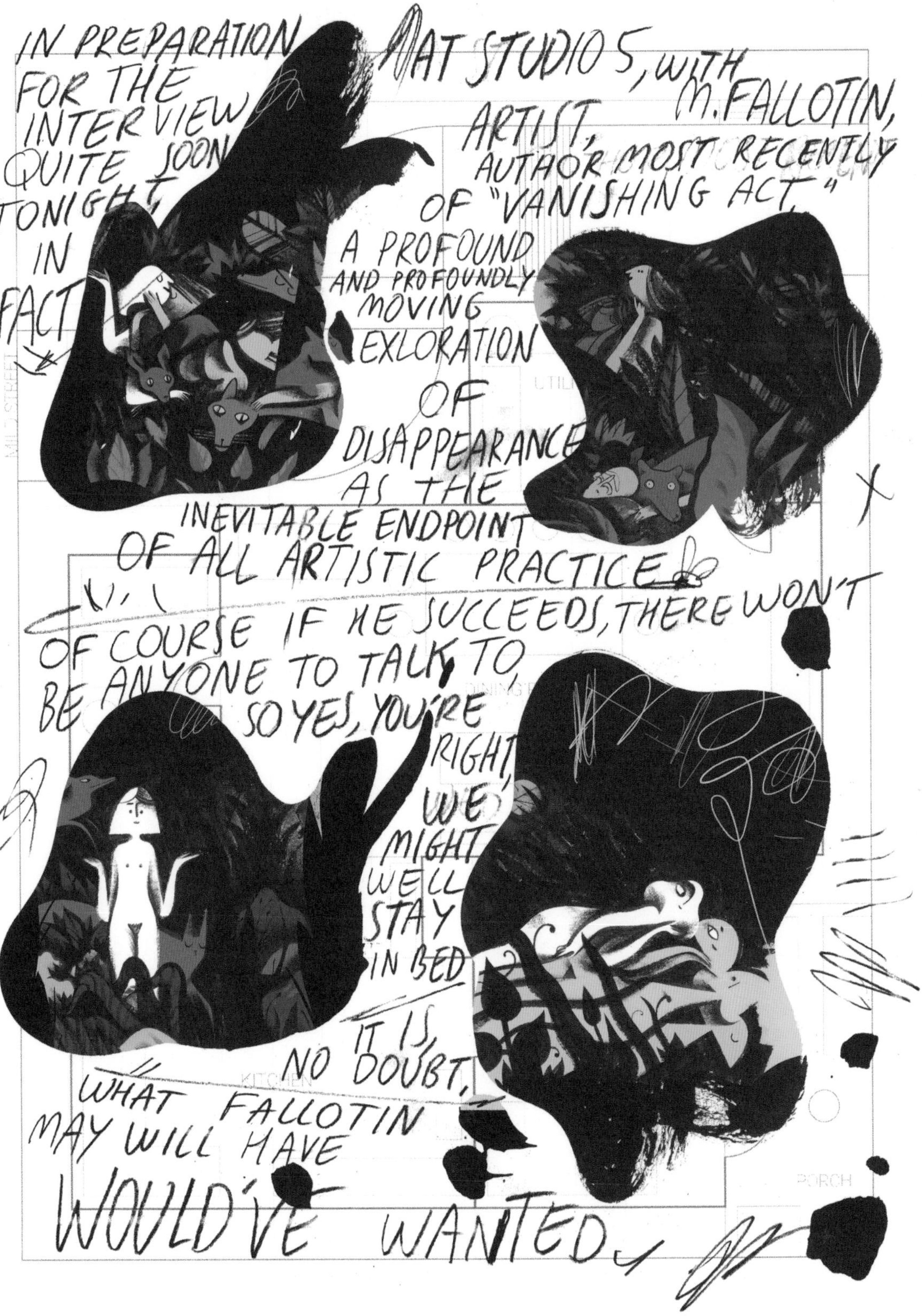
IN PREPARATION FOR THE INTERVIEW QUITE SOON TONIGHT, IN FACT
AT STUDIO 5, WITH M. FALLOTIN, ARTIST, AUTHOR MOST RECENTLY OF "VANISHING ACT," A PROFOUND AND PROFOUNDLY MOVING EXLORATION OF DISAPPEARANCE AS THE INEVITABLE ENDPOINT OF ALL ARTISTIC PRACTICE
OF COURSE IF HE SUCCEEDS, THERE WON'T BE ANYONE TO TALK TO, SO YES, YOU'RE RIGHT, WE MIGHT WELL STAY IN BED
IT IS, NO DOUBT, WHAT FALLOTIN MAY WILL HAVE WOULD'VE WANTED
MILL STREET
KITCHEN
PORCH

ACT 6
Awakenings

CAST
Simon B.

SCENE
Simon B.'s apartment
Simon B.'s daydream

TIME
22:30-22:50

And the man Peter awoke
To rehearse within his mind of minds
The impending dinner party and all of its
Embarassments multitudinously engorged

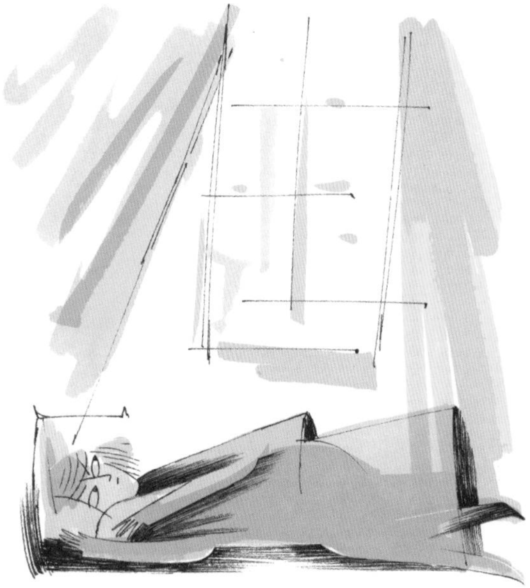

And his colleagues awoke to contemplate
The lineaments of sitcom sets within a
Coffeeshop that doubles as a laundromat that
Doubles as a dungeon that doubles as a bar

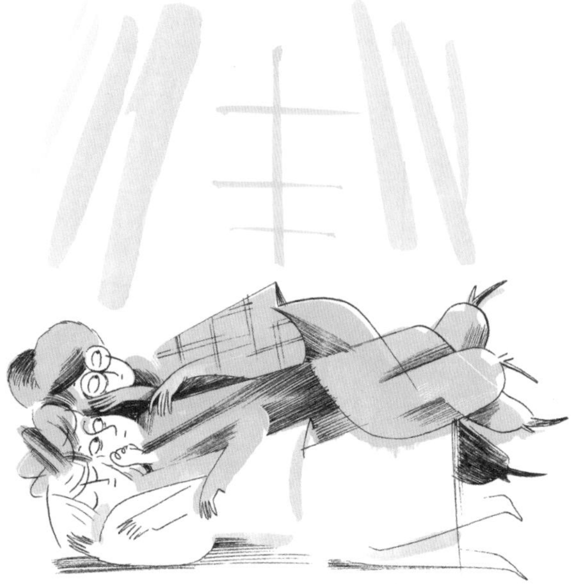

And a chance couple awoke to confer on
The subjects of everything and nothing,
And everything everything and
Everything everything everything everything

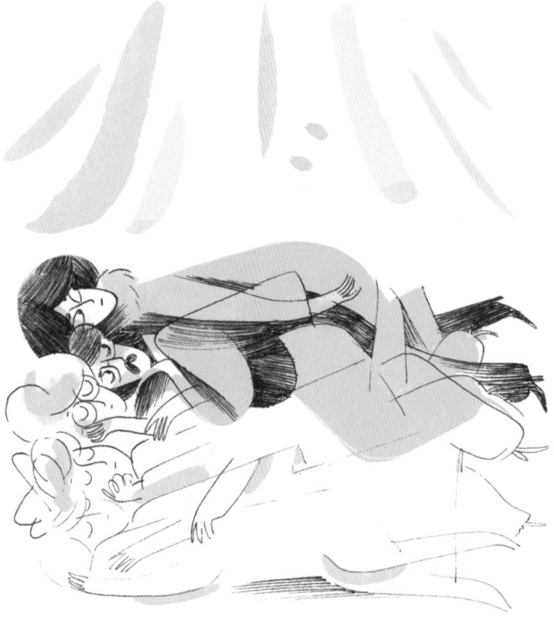

And Valerie, a thespian of moderate renown,
Awoke to part the shades of servitude and
Domination, and prune between them
Olives, dates and other forms of disaffection

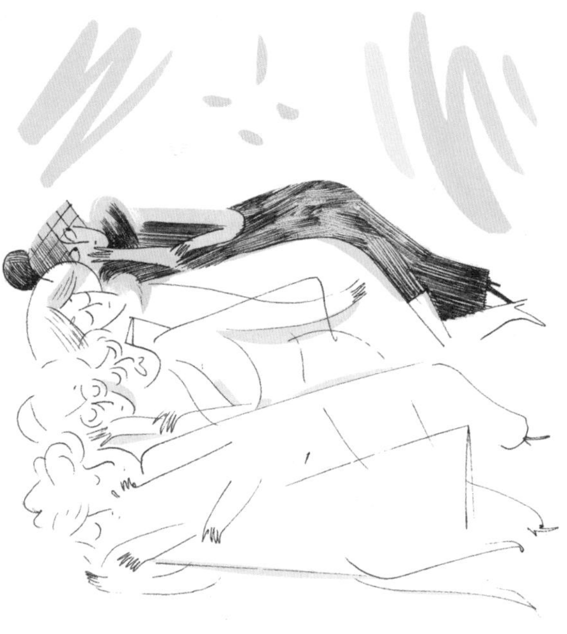

And a chance couple awoke again
To walk the lofty halls of Blatteroid's estate,
On which a change of hearts occured
Expediating class ingestion

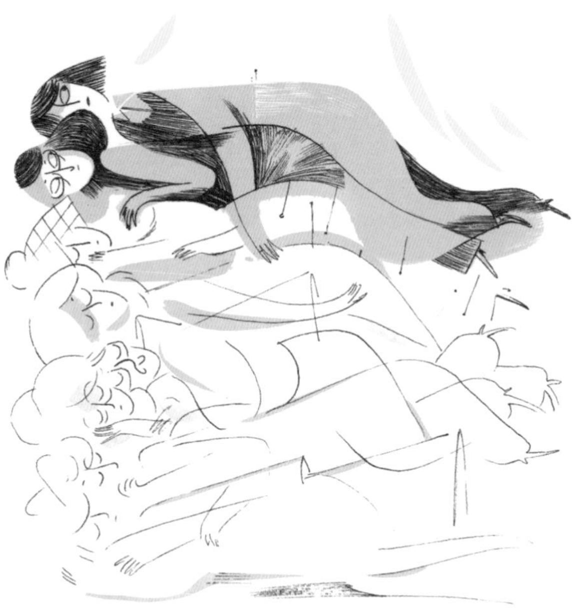

And the street awoke to dream itself
Into the night, unblinking and alone,
Reeled back and forth, and for a stretch
Suspended in the middle

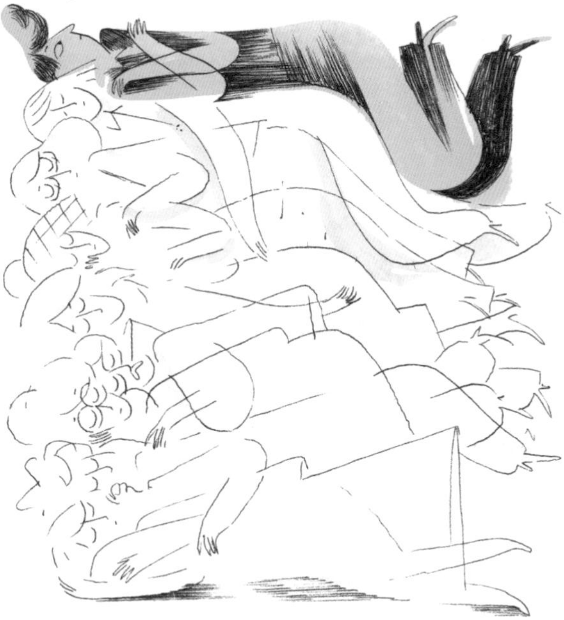

And the man Gerald awoke
To flood the universe with bile, and sail
The wakened street in search of Blatteroid,
And Fallotin and someone named Simon

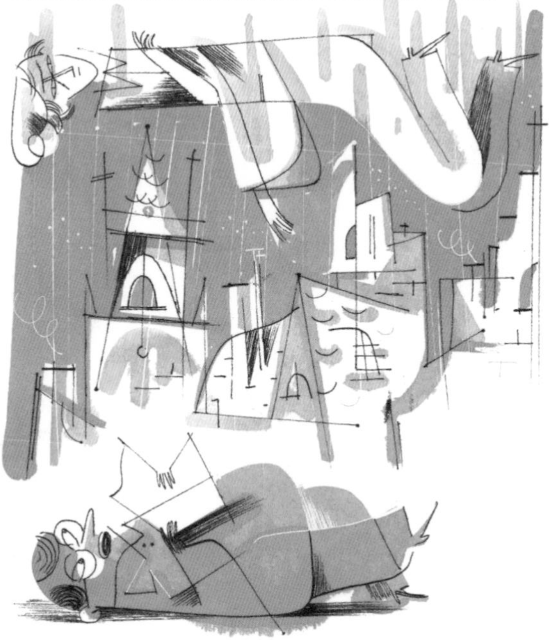

And the man Simon awoke against his will
To songs of muddled gravity,
Reprised out of his teens with
Chamberchoired insouciance

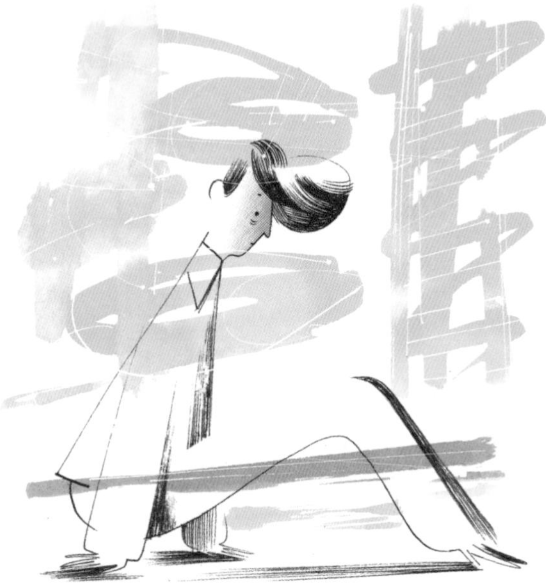

And the man Simon awoke into a tenderness
Like that of light, unorthodox to say the least,
Considering the relative maturity
Of this ungodly hour

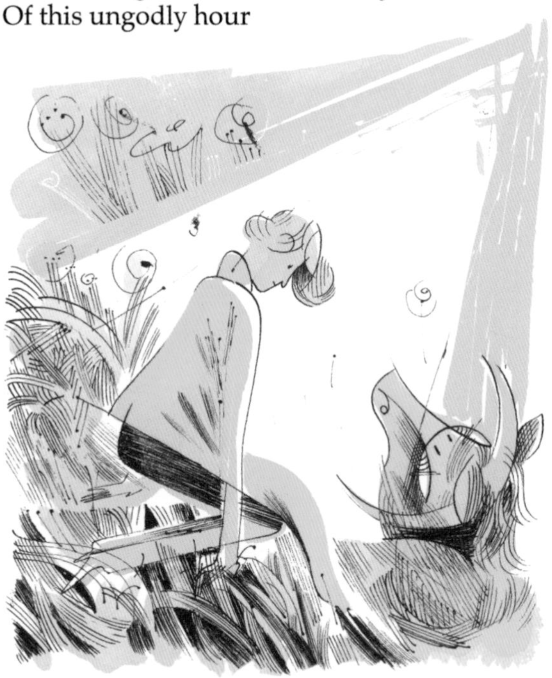

And the man Simon awoke again to find
His room transformed as in a dream
Into a memory theater
Of last night's social hours

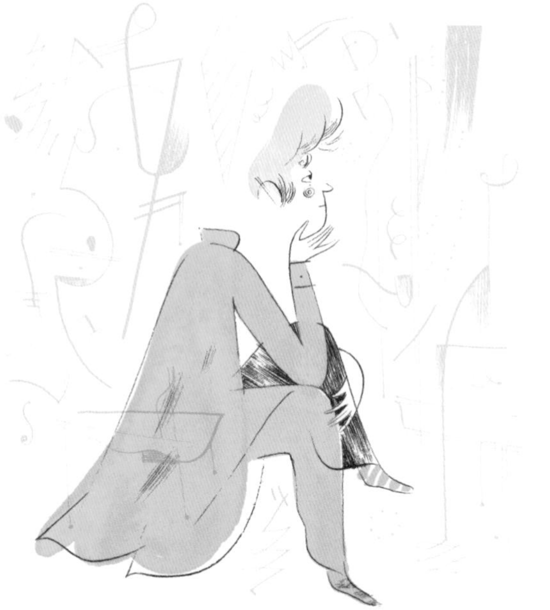

And the man Simon awoke again again
Into a semaphore in sound, and so,
Beiged up and bruised with poetry,
He dressed himself and stepped outside

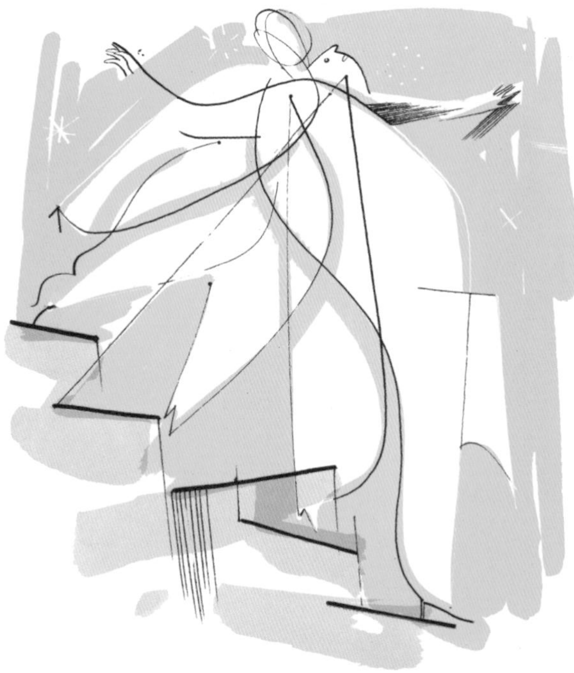

And the dog Barko awoke to smell
The nullities of humanly potential,
Paraded in a branching stream
Before his moist and brittle muzzle

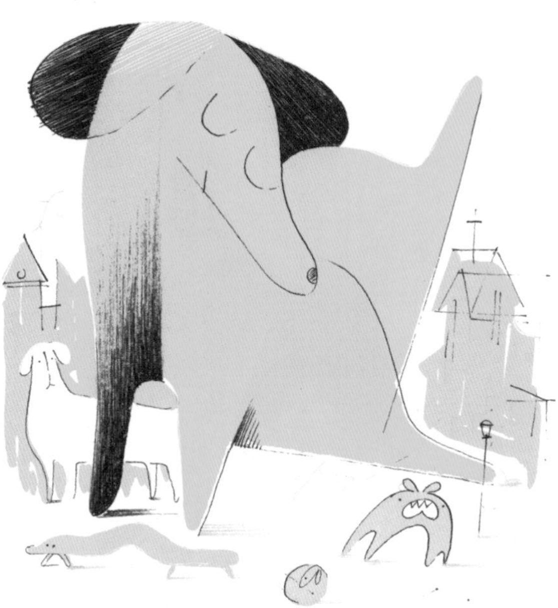

And the man Simon awoke into
Monastic robes and led the man Gerald
Into an improvised confession, which left
The two unbonded, more even than before

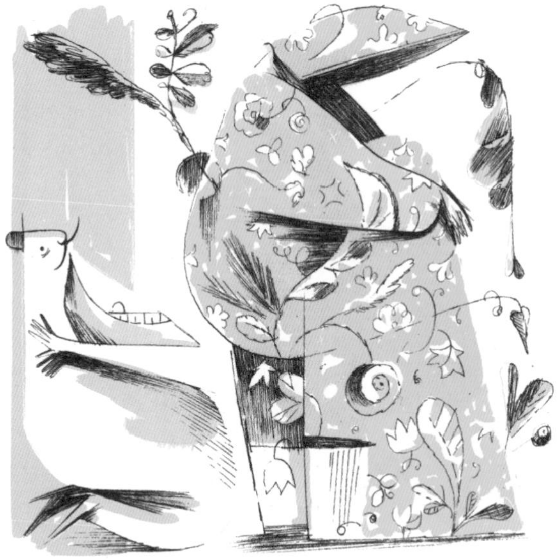

And Studio 5's monitors awoke into
A panoply of recommissioned shows,
Together stitched in arbitrary,
Yet unerring order

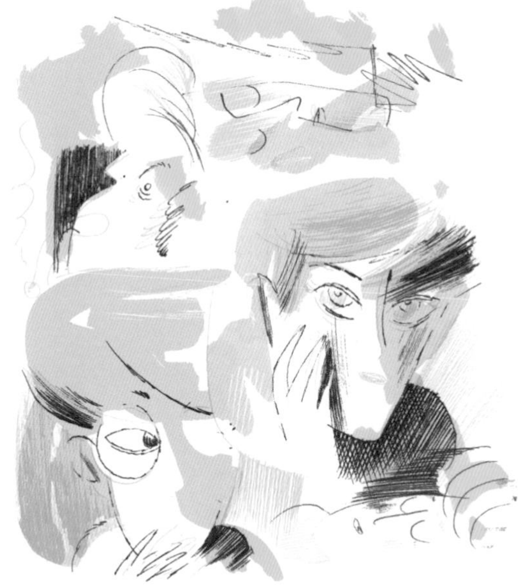

And the man Fallotin awoke to guide the man
Blatteroid, or rather his replacement, through
Something called "Vanishing Act," deliriously
Vague with or without interpretation

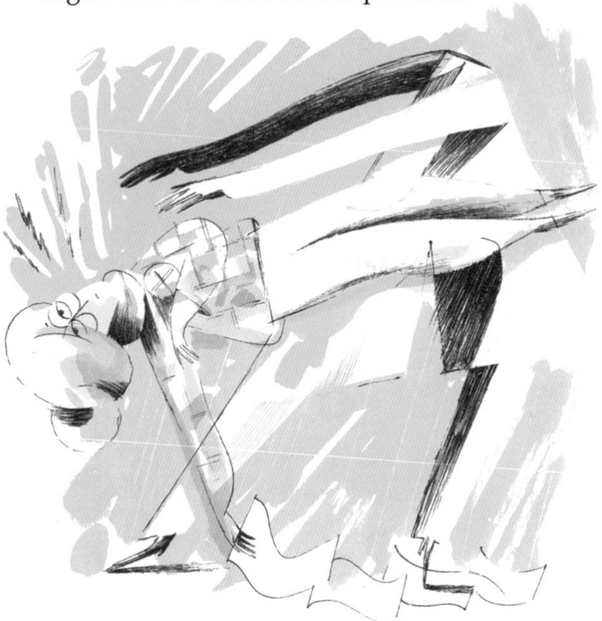

And the woman Sybil awoke to entertain
Her guests, some of who, all of who,
That is to say, or none to be precise,
Could bother to be present

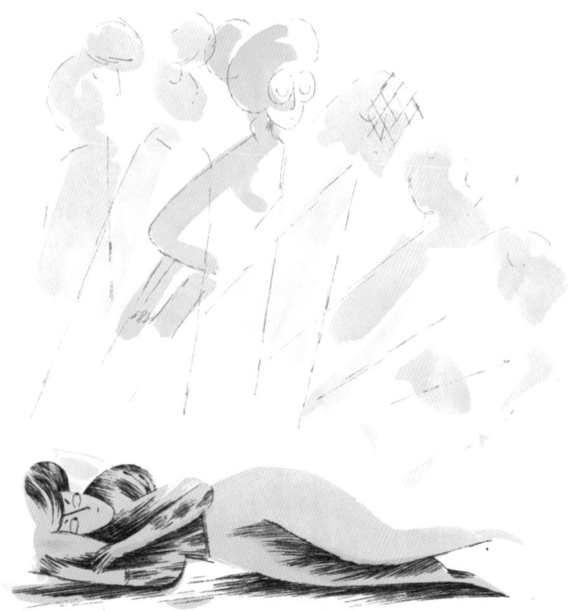

ACT 7
Wandering Vox

CAST
Belinda C.
Gerald Bland
T. B.
Val Fran R.
F. Premise
Simon B.
Madeleine F.
G. A.
M. Fallotin

SCENE
Mild Street
Studio 5, recording studio

TIME
22:40-23:00

Well, it's a mild Thursday evening and Gerald Bland, producer of the Weekly Browlift, is fuming down the stairs of Studio 5 in search of tonight's interviewer, interviewee, and operator.

The program's regular presenter, Slats Blatteroid, seems to have improvised for himself a vacation immediately following the one he'd just returned from.

As usual, Bland resigns himself to pick a replacement among the promenading crowds of the Art District.

Being the first person Bland bumps into, Studio 5's generously haired Production Coordinator qualifies as a temporary host, a position she accepts with guarded enthusiasm.

Accompanying her is Valerie Fran R., a part-time elm-and-pine impersonator, increasingly out of demand in this dark age of CGI, green screens and polyester trees, and barkish leafy rooted trees, and all such verdant simulations.

And so, the three of them proceed across the road to wake the camera operator, habitually asleep at any given hour.

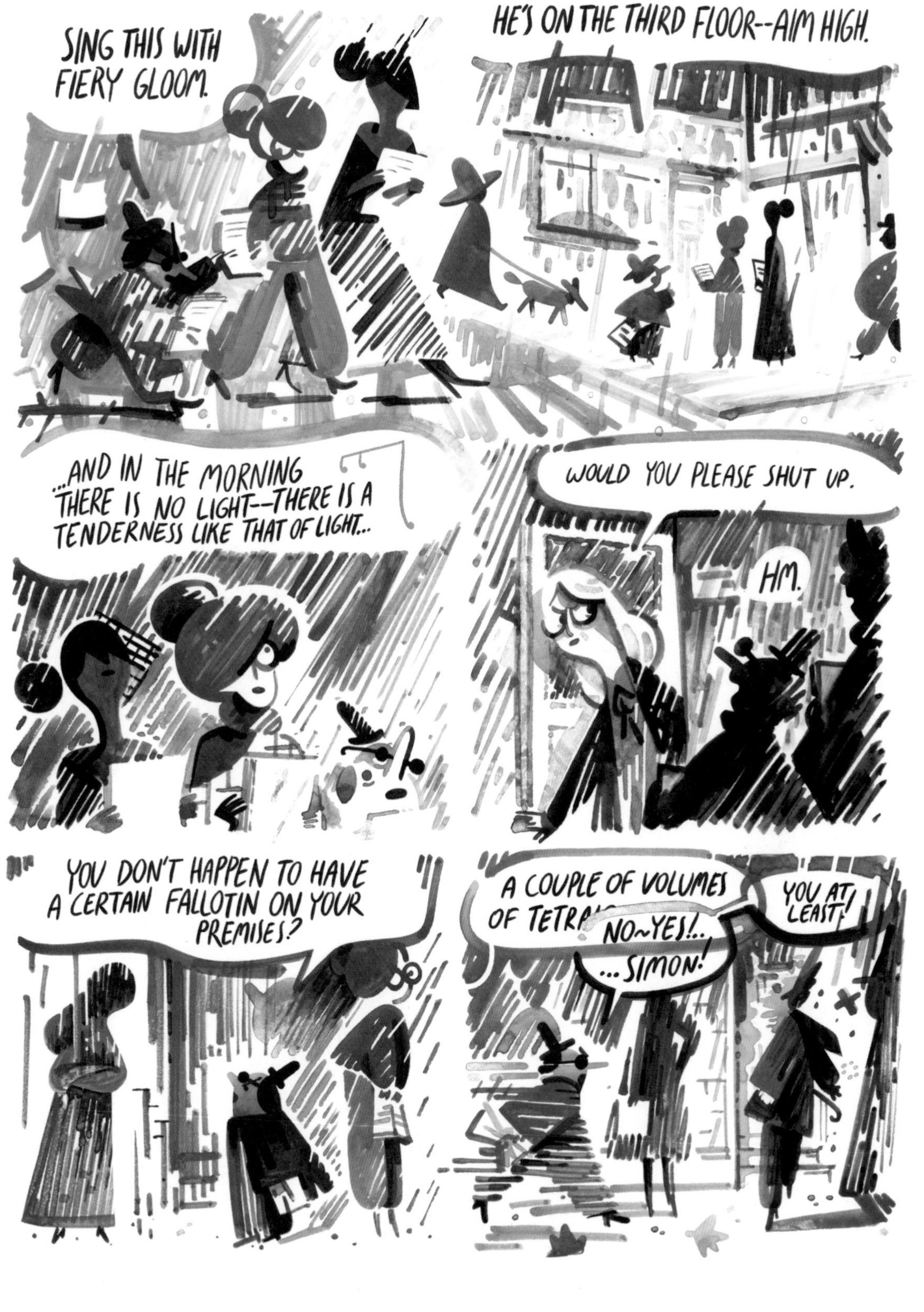
SING THIS WITH FIERY GLOOM.
HE'S ON THE THIRD FLOOR--AIM HIGH.
...AND IN THE MORNING THERE IS NO LIGHT--THERE IS A TENDERNESS LIKE THAT OF LIGHT...
WOULD YOU PLEASE SHUT UP.
HM.
YOU DON'T HAPPEN TO HAVE A CERTAIN FALLOTIN ON YOUR PREMISES?
A COUPLE OF VOLUMES OF TETRA
NO~YES!..
...SIMON!
YOU AT LEAST!

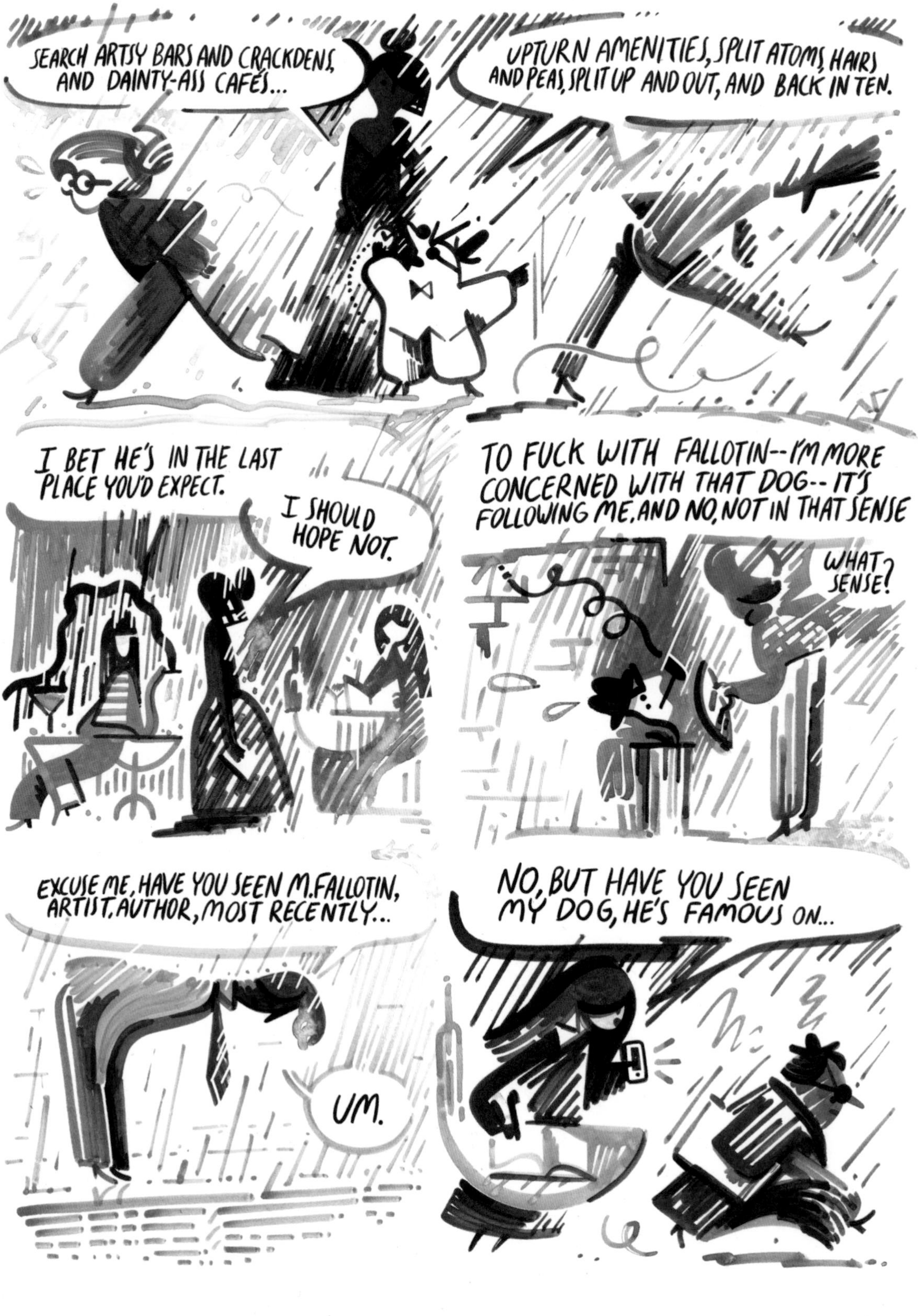
SEARCH ARTSY BARS AND CRACKDENS, AND DAINTY-ASS CAFÉS...
UPTURN AMENITIES, SPLIT ATOMS, HAIRS AND PEAS, SPLIT UP AND OUT, AND BACK IN TEN.
I BET HE'S IN THE LAST PLACE YOU'D EXPECT.
I SHOULD HOPE NOT.
TO FUCK WITH FALLOTIN--I'M MORE CONCERNED WITH THAT DOG-- IT'S FOLLOWING ME, AND NO, NOT IN THAT SENSE
WHAT SENSE?
EXCUSE ME, HAVE YOU SEEN M.FALLOTIN, ARTIST, AUTHOR, MOST RECENTLY...
UM.
NO, BUT HAVE YOU SEEN MY DOG, HE'S FAMOUS ON...

Bland hadn't seen my dog, or else he couldn't spare a moment to reply.

Instead, he returned to the studio,
chanting the F word like a summoning spell.

Somehow, somewhat, it worked, though Fallotin was quick to contest

any notion of the supernatural by claiming he'd come
to the studio early, as instructed.

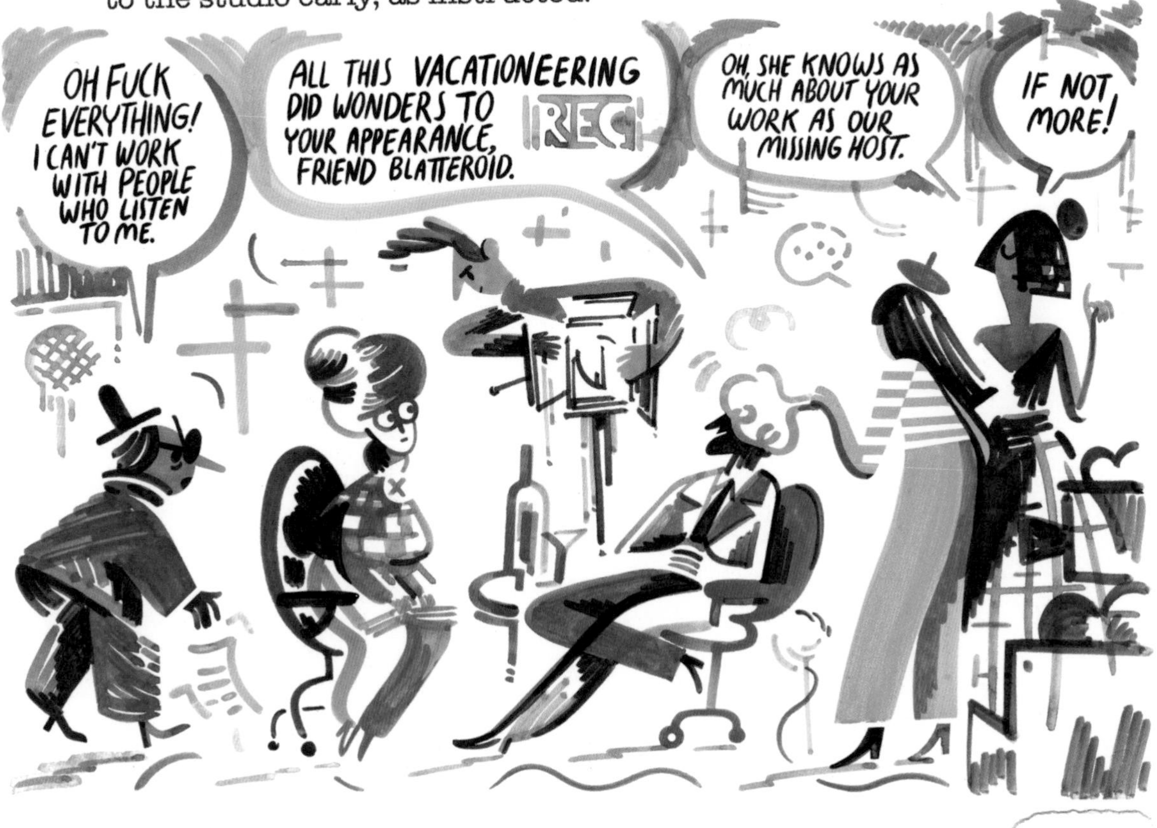
OH FUCK EVERYTHING! I CAN'T WORK WITH PEOPLE WHO LISTEN TO ME.
ALL THIS VACATIONEERING DID WONDERS TO YOUR APPEARANCE, FRIEND BLATTEROID.
REC
OH, SHE KNOWS AS MUCH ABOUT YOUR WORK AS OUR MISSING HOST.
IF NOT MORE!

With this I end my dispatch from the street, twice manifold in its vicinity,
and recommence the search for my dear dog, twice previously mentioned.

And if you see him, please let him know that I miss all aspects of his
dogged self, and I will give up gladly this anointed omnipresence
to grasp again through seethrough polystyrene the softness of his stool.

PS. There is a dinner party I might attend later, but no, I definitely won't,
and neither will nobody

ACT 8
The Seagull and the Void

CAST
Simon B.
Robert B.
Gerald Bland

SCENE
Simon B.'s apartment
the Last Street
Studio 5, recording studio

TIME
22:50-23:10

In the beginning there was nothing.

Nothing save for a lone seagull soaring across the void.

Over the course of eternity the void grew tiresome.

So the seagull went and shat it all out.

And now we 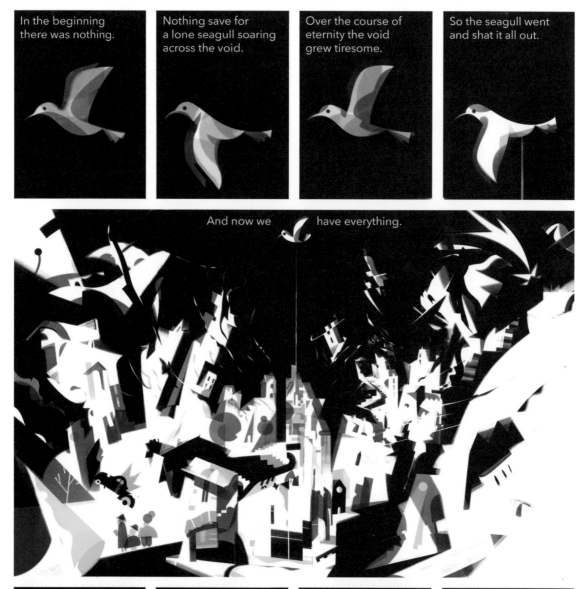 have everything.

Central heating, pronouns,

the music of Gerald Gibraltar and the Dubrovnicks,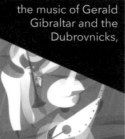

aubergines, diffusion, a man named Simon,

and a lamppost for the seagull to perch upon.

The man Simon is tormented by:

1. A persistent hangover.

2. Exceedingly callous coworkers.

3. A certain hymn that had awoken him this evening.

The latter is an invention of Simon's uncle Bob,

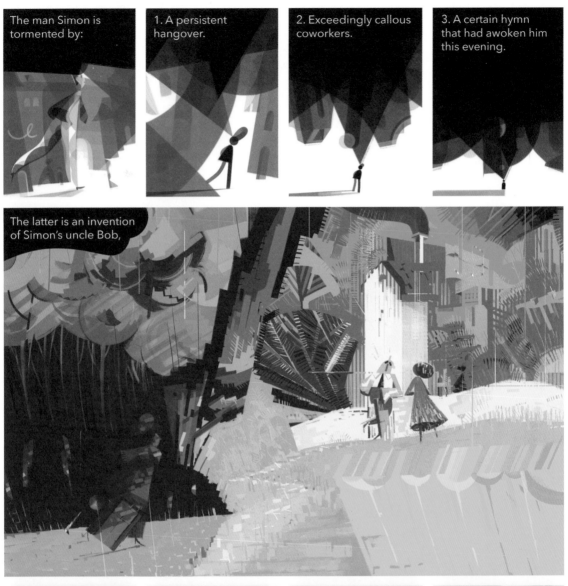

a retired combustion engine repairman

who owned a not entirely charmless summerhouse south of the city

and had a habit of field-testing all his poetic concoctions

on his unwitting guests

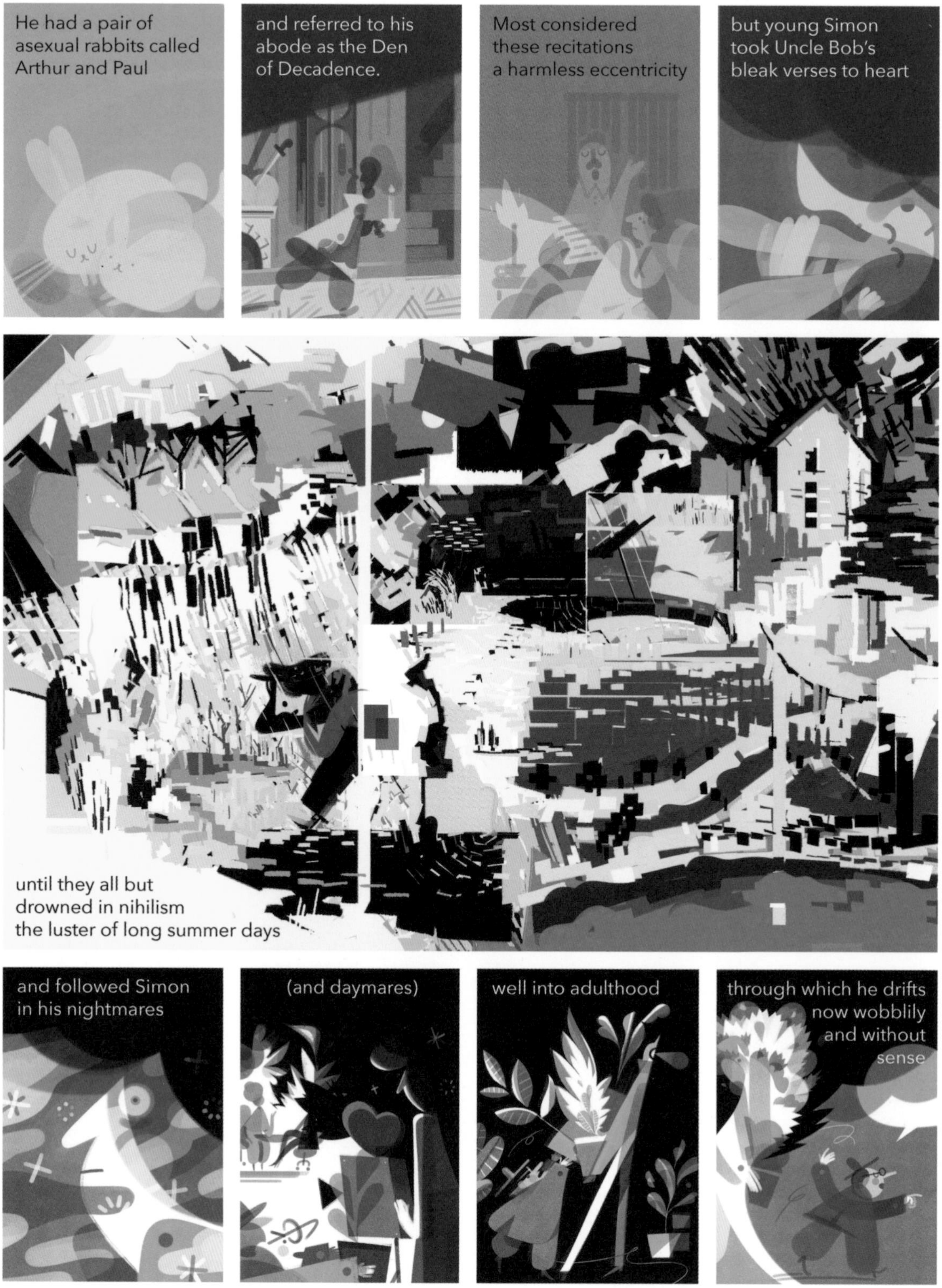
He had a pair of
asexual rabbits called
Arthur and Paul
and referred to his
abode as the Den
of Decadence.
Most considered
these recitations
a harmless eccentricity
but young Simon
took Uncle Bob's
bleak verses to heart
until they all but
drowned in nihilism
the luster of long summer days
and followed Simon
in his nightmares
(and daymares)
well into adulthood
through which he drifts
now wobblily
and without
sense

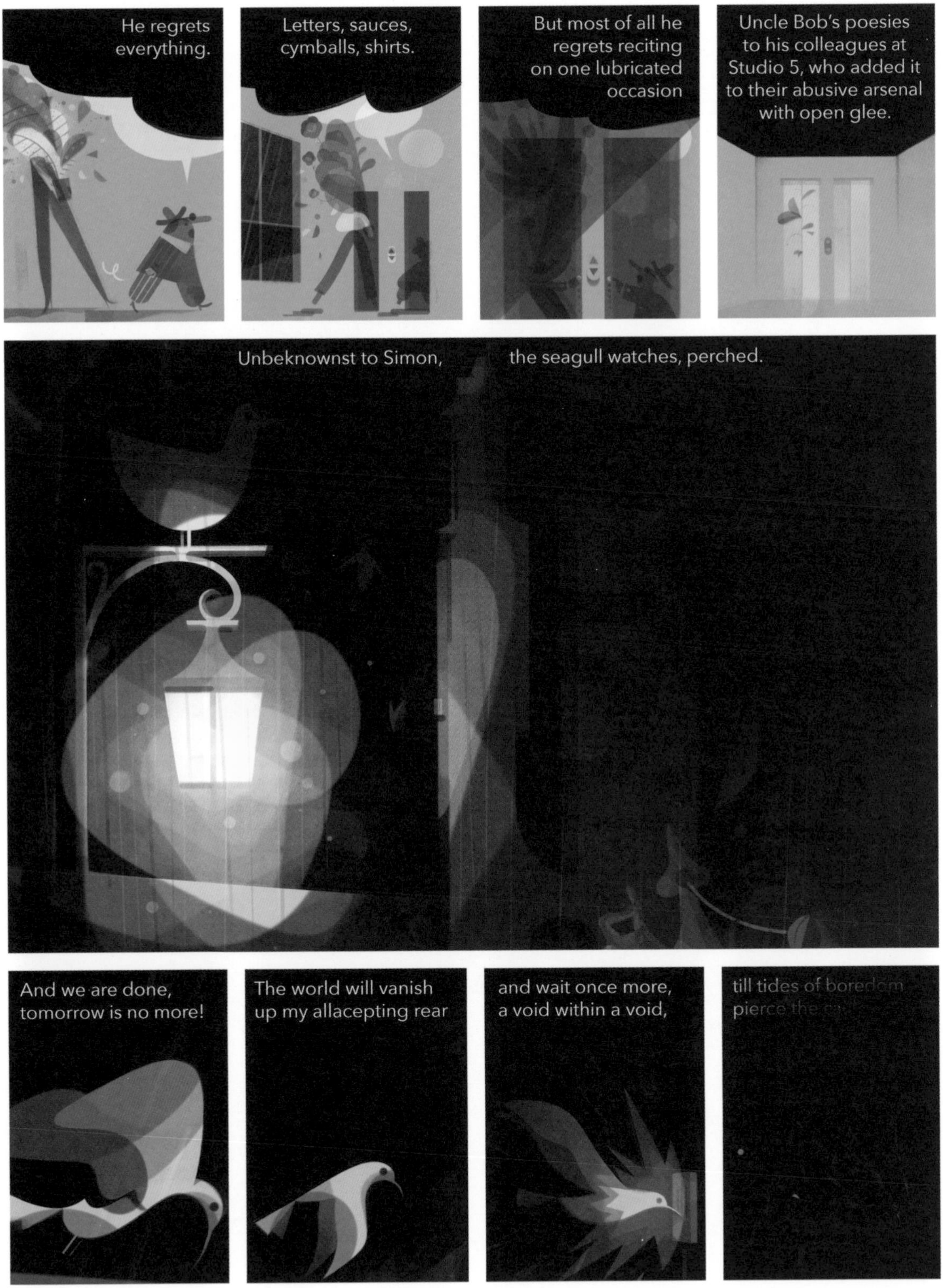

He regrets everything.

Letters, sauces, cymballs, shirts.

But most of all he regrets reciting on one lubricated occasion

Uncle Bob's poesies to his colleagues at Studio 5, who added it to their abusive arsenal with open glee.

Unbeknownst to Simon, the seagull watches, perched.

And we are done, tomorrow is no more!

The world will vanish up my allaccepting rear

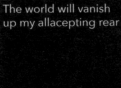

and wait once more, a void within a void,

till tides of boredom pierce the ear

ACT 9
The Barko Continuum

CAST
Gerald Bland
M. Fallotin
Val Fran R.
Madeleine F.
T. B.
Simon B.
Belinda C.
G.A.
Barko

SCENE
Studio 5, green room

TIME
23:00-23:20

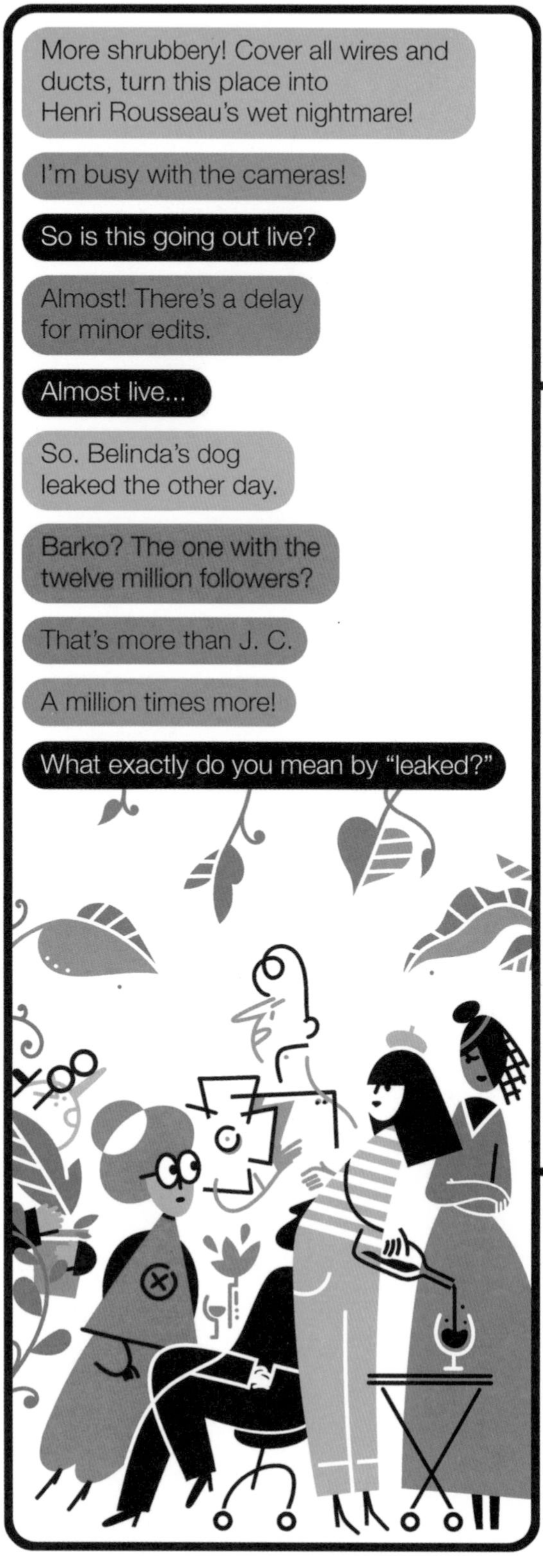
More shrubbery! Cover all wires and ducts, turn this place into Henri Rousseau's wet nightmare!
I'm busy with the cameras!
So is this going out live?
Almost! There's a delay for minor edits.
Almost live...
So. Belinda's dog leaked the other day.
Barko? The one with the twelve million followers?
That's more than J. C.
A million times more!
What exactly do you mean by "leaked?"

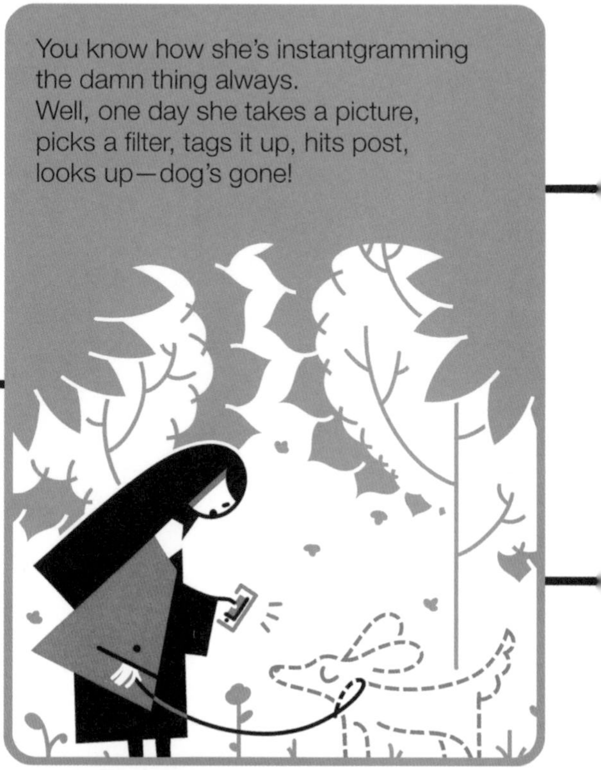
You know how she's instantgramming the damn thing always.
Well, one day she takes a picture, picks a filter, tags it up, hits post, looks up—dog's gone!

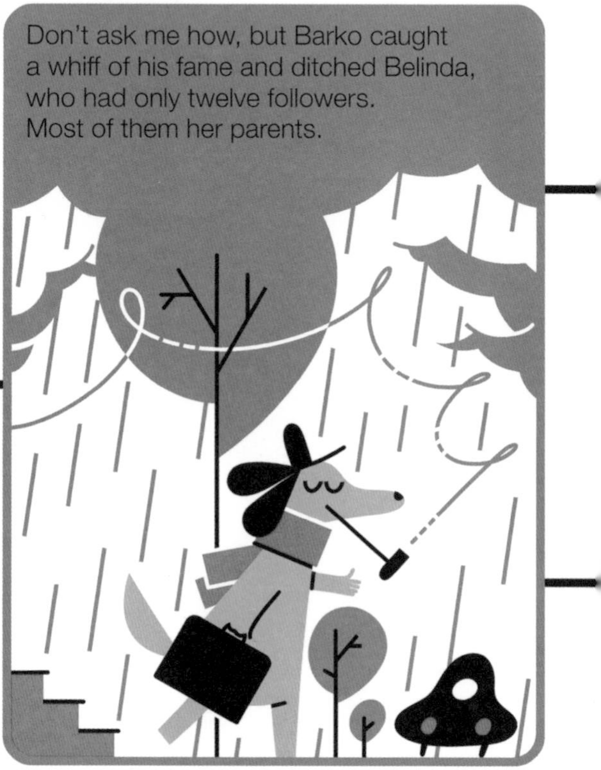
Don't ask me how, but Barko caught a whiff of his fame and ditched Belinda, who had only twelve followers.
Most of them her parents.

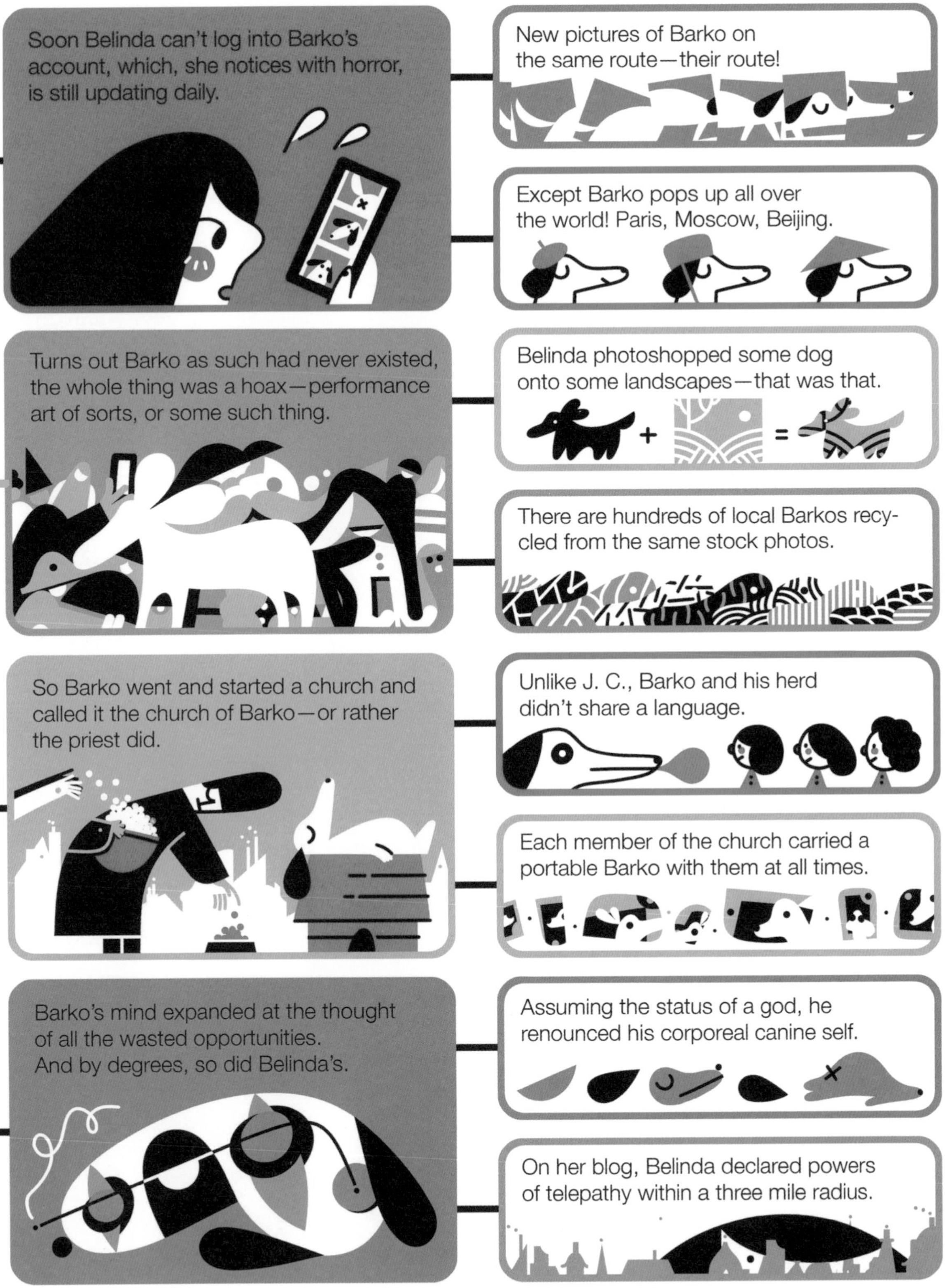
Soon Belinda can't log into Barko's account, which, she notices with horror, is still updating daily.
New pictures of Barko on the same route—their route!
Except Barko pops up all over the world! Paris, Moscow, Beijing.
Turns out Barko as such had never existed, the whole thing was a hoax—performance art of sorts, or some such thing.
Belinda photoshopped some dog onto some landscapes—that was that.
+
=
There are hundreds of local Barkos recycled from the same stock photos.
So Barko went and started a church and called it the church of Barko—or rather the priest did.
Unlike J. C., Barko and his herd didn't share a language.
Each member of the church carried a portable Barko with them at all times.
Barko's mind expanded at the thought of all the wasted opportunities. And by degrees, so did Belinda's.
Assuming the status of a god, he renounced his corporeal canine self.
On her blog, Belinda declared powers of telepathy within a three mile radius.

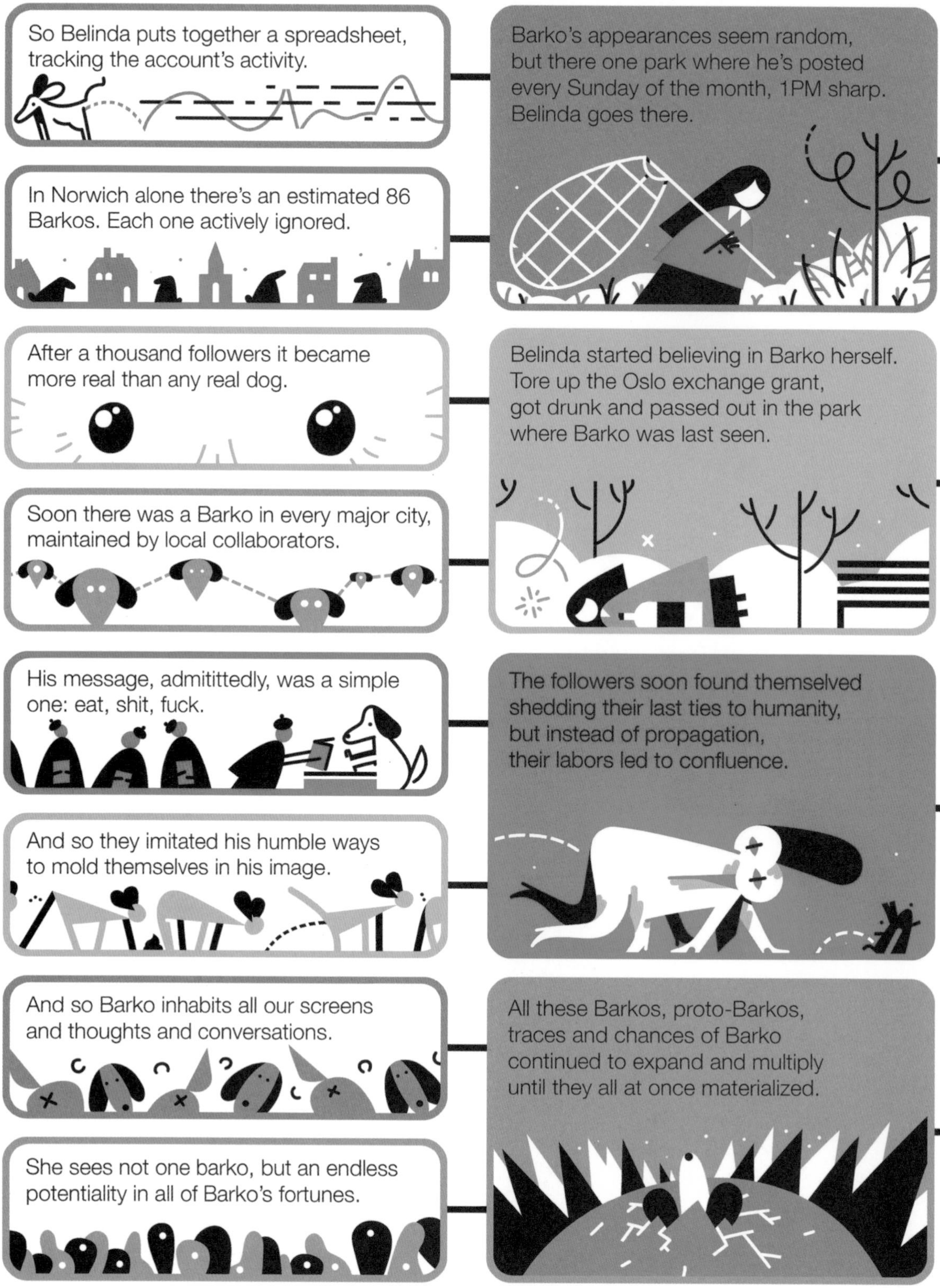

So Belinda puts together a spreadsheet, tracking the account's activity.
In Norwich alone there's an estimated 86 Barkos. Each one actively ignored.
After a thousand followers it became more real than any real dog.
Soon there was a Barko in every major city, maintained by local collaborators.
His message, admitittedly, was a simple one: eat, shit, fuck.
And so they imitated his humble ways to mold themselves in his image.
And so Barko inhabits all our screens and thoughts and conversations.
She sees not one barko, but an endless potentiality in all of Barko's fortunes.
Barko's appearances seem random, but there one park where he's posted every Sunday of the month, 1PM sharp. Belinda goes there.
Belinda started believing in Barko herself. Tore up the Oslo exchange grant, got drunk and passed out in the park where Barko was last seen.
The followers soon found themselved shedding their last ties to humanity, but instead of propagation, their labors led to confluence.
All these Barkos, proto-Barkos, traces and chances of Barko continued to expand and multiply until they all at once materialized.

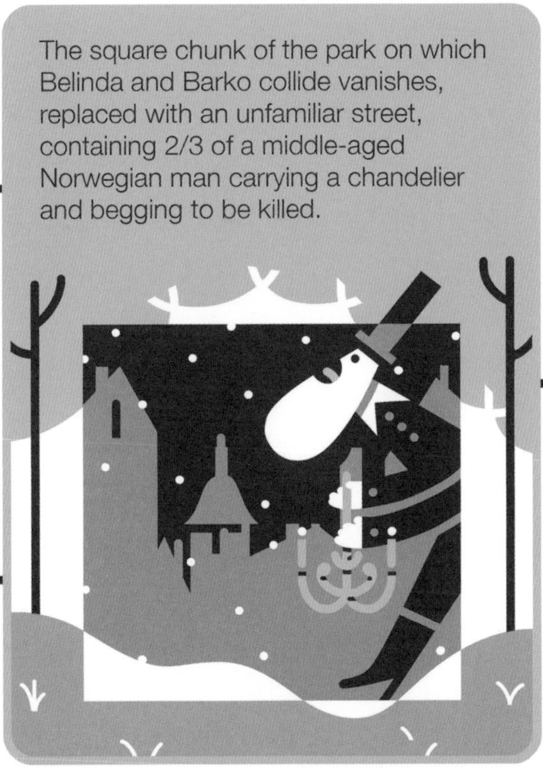
The square chunk of the park on which Belinda and Barko collide vanishes, replaced with an unfamiliar street, containing 2/3 of a middle-aged Norwegian man carrying a chandelier and begging to be killed.

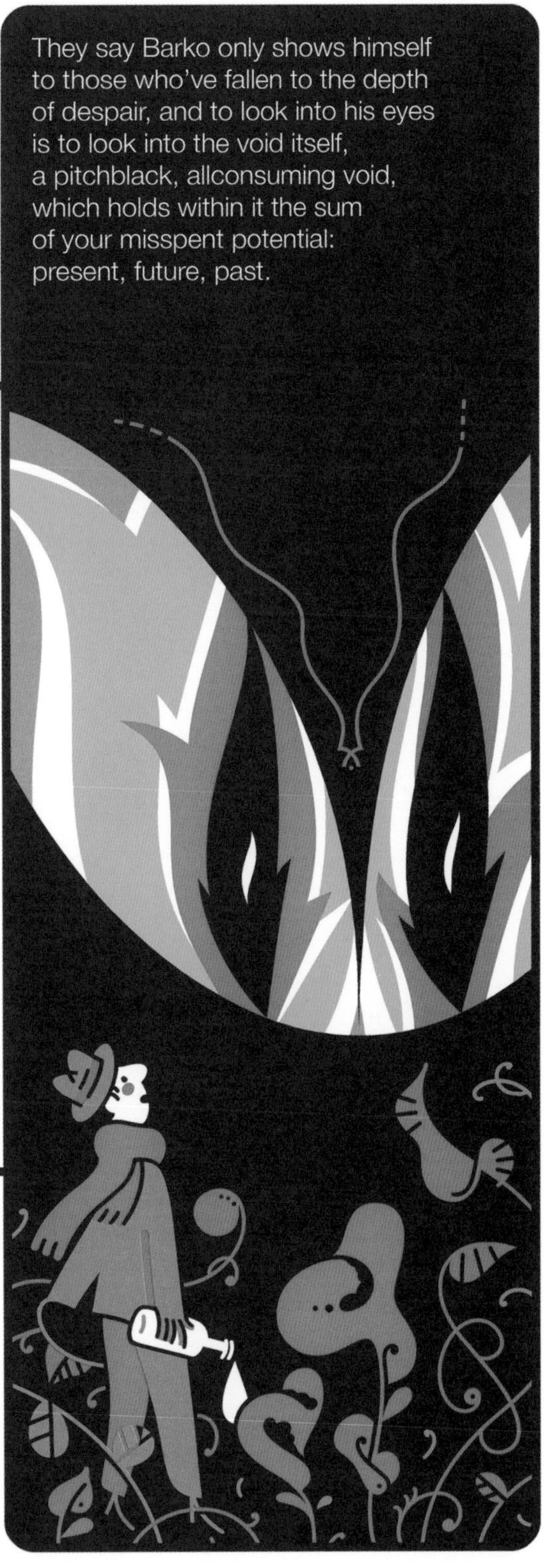
They say Barko only shows himself to those who've fallen to the depth of despair, and to look into his eyes is to look into the void itself, a pitchblack, allconsuming void, which holds within it the sum of your misspent potential: present, future, past.

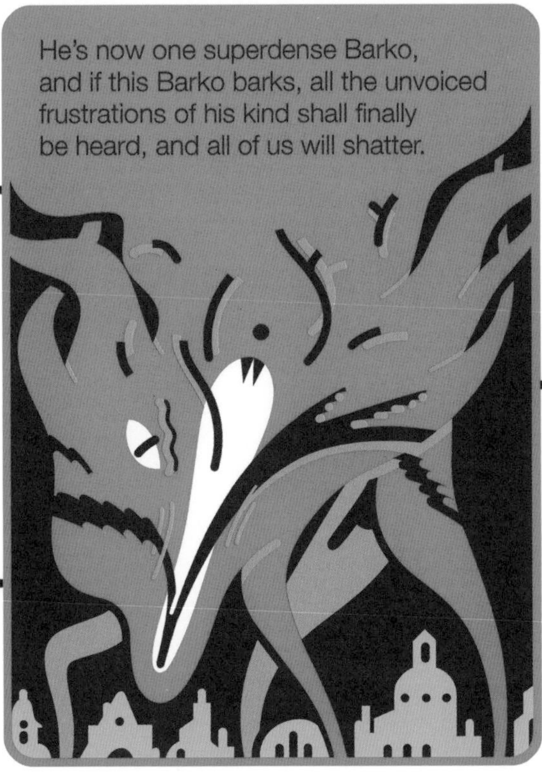
He's now one superdense Barko, and if this Barko barks, all the unvoiced frustrations of his kind shall finally be heard, and all of us will shatter.

ACT 10
Elevator Machinery

CAST
Gerald Bland
Simon B.

SCENE
Studio 5, elevators
Studio 5, control room

TIME
23:10-23:30

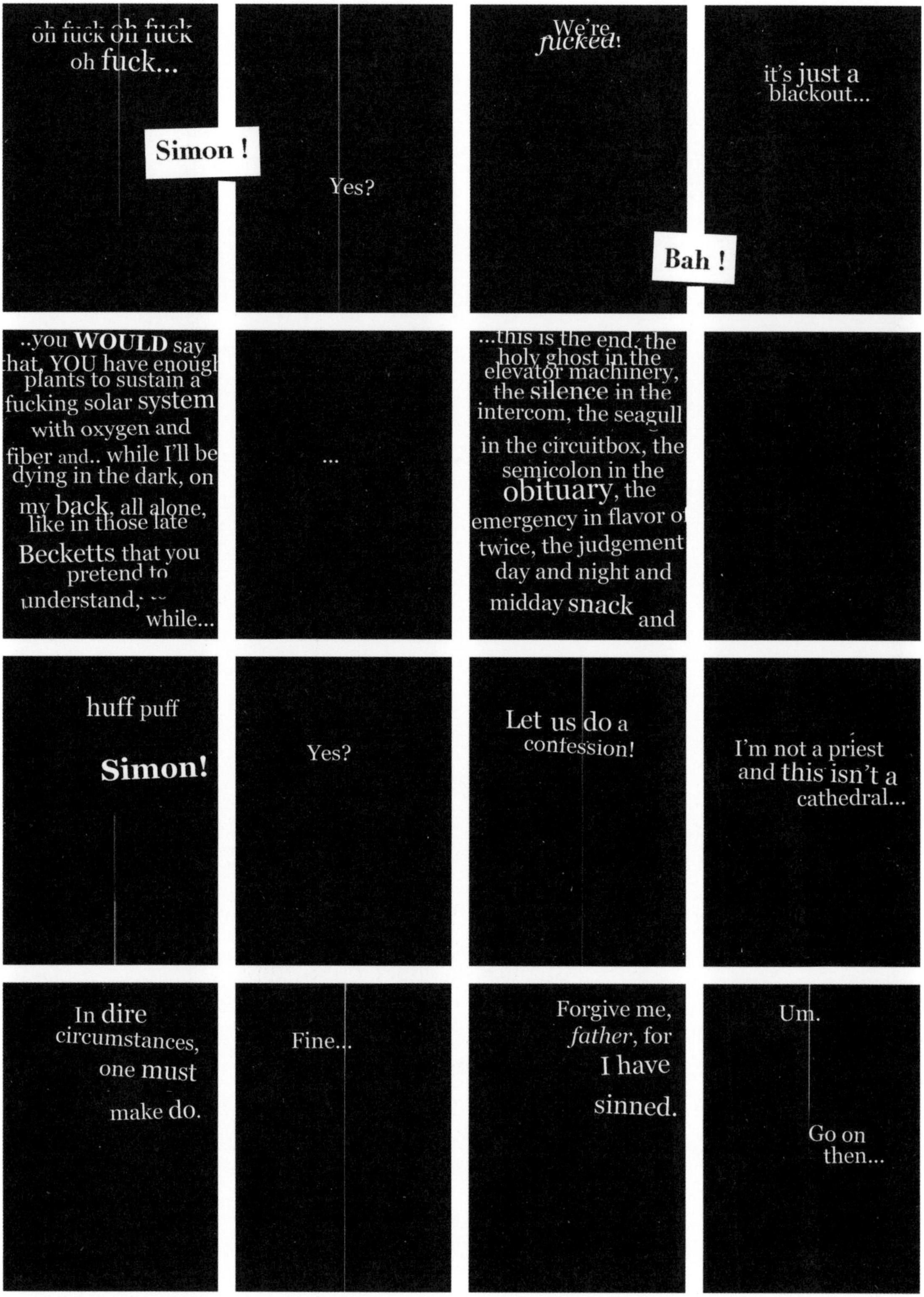
oh fuck oh fuck
oh fuck...
Simon !
Yes?
We're fucked!
Bah !
it's just a blackout...
..you WOULD say hat, YOU have enough plants to sustain a fucking solar system with oxygen and fiber and.. while I'll be dying in the dark, on my back, all alone, like in those late Becketts that you pretend to understand, while...
...
...this is the end, the holy ghost in the elevator machinery, the silence in the intercom, the seagull in the circuitbox, the semicolon in the obituary, the emergency in flavor of twice, the judgement day and night and midday snack and
huff puff
Simon!
Yes?
Let us do a confession!
I'm not a priest and this isn't a cathedral...
In dire circumstances, one must make do.
Fine...
Forgive me, father, for I have sinned.
Um.
Go on then...

Where to begin..
Well,
Your salary has been *somewhat* adjusted to reflect my opinion of your coiffure.

I though Shut it, Simon
it was to d This is my
with my.. confession
Where was I.
Right, carnal sins!
Oh god in heaven, the numbering of wives I've fucked

It's decimal to the extreme! even fucked my own, and Blatteroid's, and yours, although you haven't got one, her ox his cupboards and their vents, and pipes and pins and next: what's next? venial

Broke two Weiweis, punched a Monet, upended a Brancusi... I could go on...

in life: same, twice, queen anne'd, twice more, more lies, a string of sleepwalk murders, dear dog, I *do* regret it all!

That day I took off work and loathed myself for being unprodroductive,

the day before I wasted on the Blatteroids and all their wooly pinny kind, so similar to me it's borderline fantastic

The hours I spent with scaly things, outdated and *uncouth*, in syncopated acupuncture and laterally spent...

the stars and bodies, both heavenly and not, the land and densilating occilates, and then the plants, particularly plants

The sky, that gaping prolapse of fuck-all, at once so infinite and is that a tautology? well spotted me or oxymoron wait oh god there is no time, no space, no god but god

and all the tiresome dichotomies of days and nights, an obvious excuse to fill the sky, with stars and suns two days onwards and for beginning there remains... oh what?

One *last* thing to confess, to you, and to the whole humanity, my lowest crime my ultimate downfall, my sin, my final sentence.

sh
ccrk

rrck

oh.

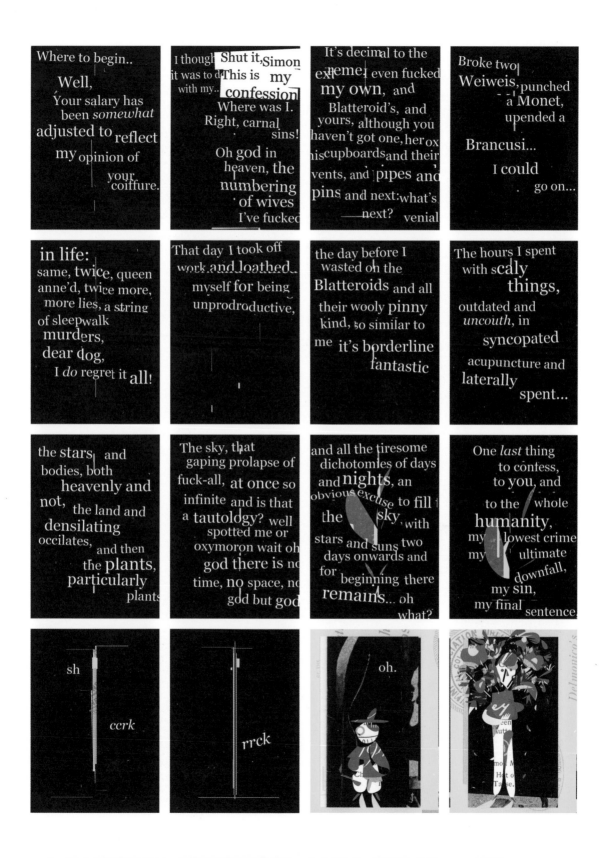

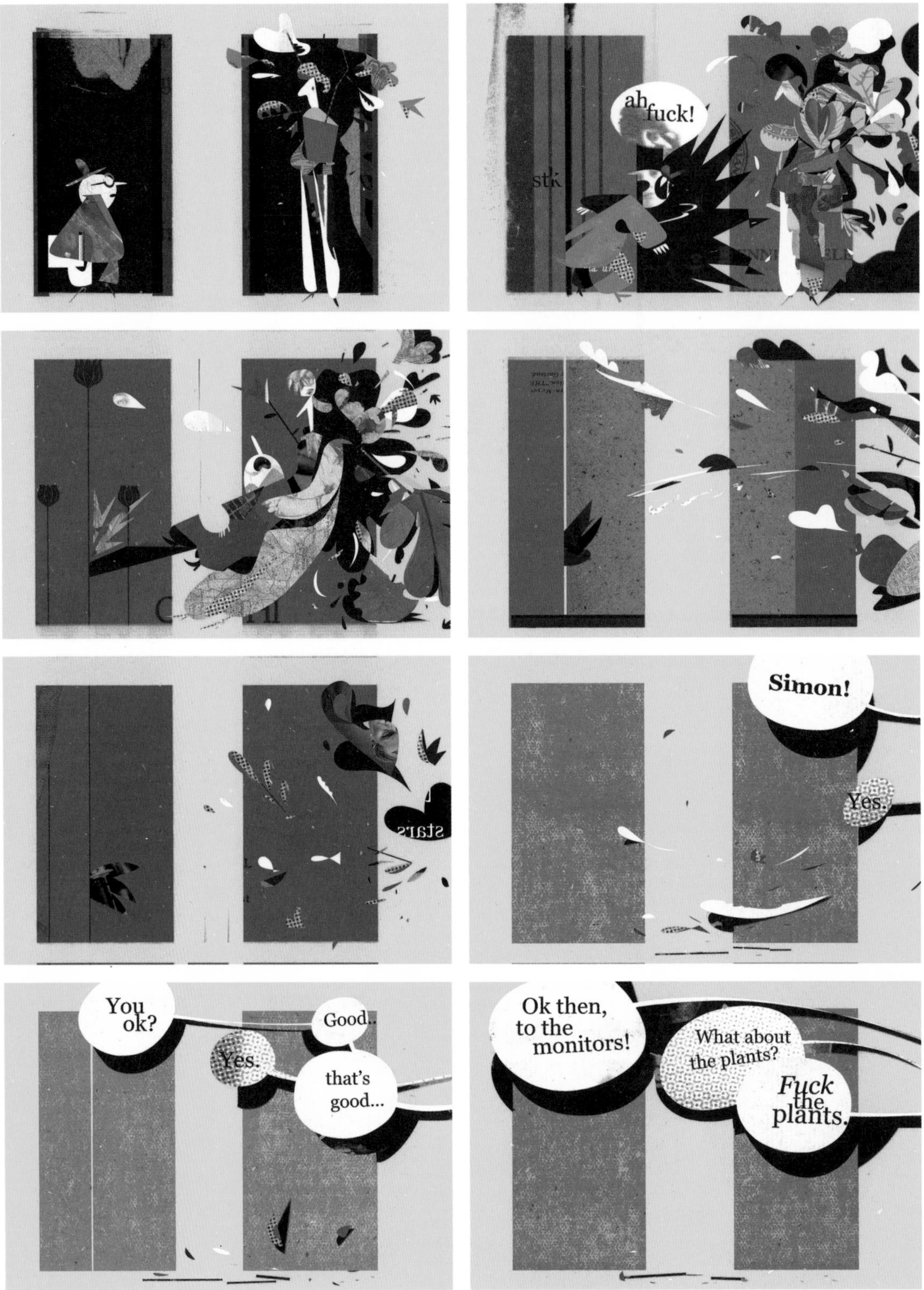
ah fuck!
Simon!
Yes.
You ok?
Yes.
Good..
that's good...
Ok then, to the monitors!
What about the plants?
Fuck the plants.

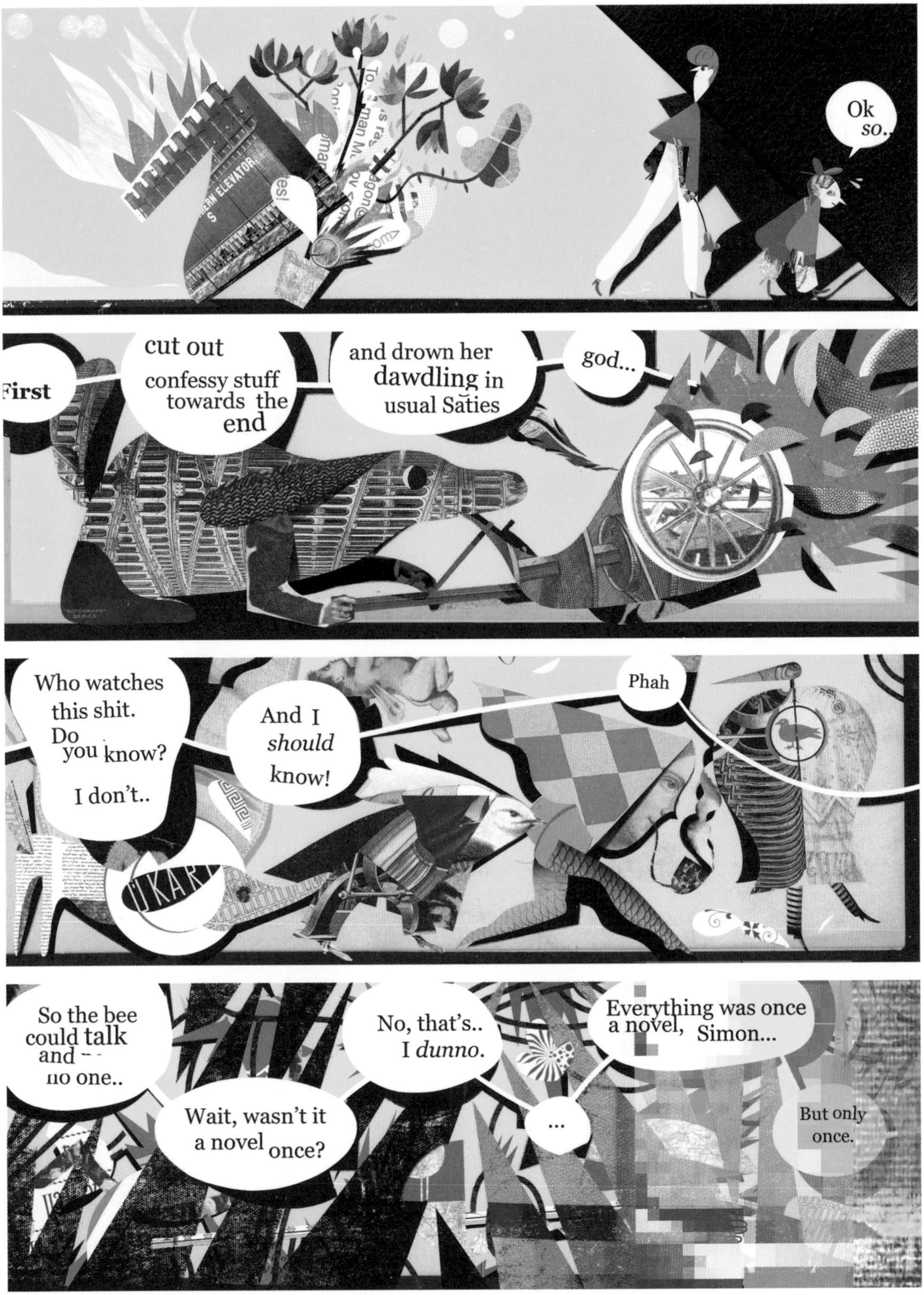
Ok so..
First
cut out confessy stuff towards the end
and drown her dawdling in usual Saties
god...
Who watches this shit. Do you know? I don't..
And I should know!
Phah
So the bee could talk and
no one..
No, that's.. I dunno.
Wait, wasn't it a novel once?
...
Everything was once a novel, Simon...
But only once.

ACT 11
Attractions! Upcoming!

CAST

Jarry in the House of Rue: Peter Hall as Jarry, G. A. as his neighbor,
Madeleine F. as his ex-lover, Robert B. as his friend.
The Daily Grime Season 12: Peter Hall as Grime Solvent, Madeleine F. as his assistant,
G. A. as the sleepwalk murderer, Val Fran R. as the judge.
A Taste of the Arts Season 4: Slats Blatteroid as the narrator.
The Beekeper: Peter Hall as the Beekeeper, G. A. as the Czar,
Madeleine F. as the Czar's daughter, Val Fran R. as the Androcles the bee.
The Quiet Lives of Robert Walser: Peter Hall as Robert Walser.
The Edge of Sebald: Val Fran R. as a dutch elm.
The Seagull: Sybil Same as Nina.
The Weekly Browlift: T. B. as Slats Blatteroid, M. Fallotin as himself.

SCENE
Studio 5, archives

TIME
23:20–23:40

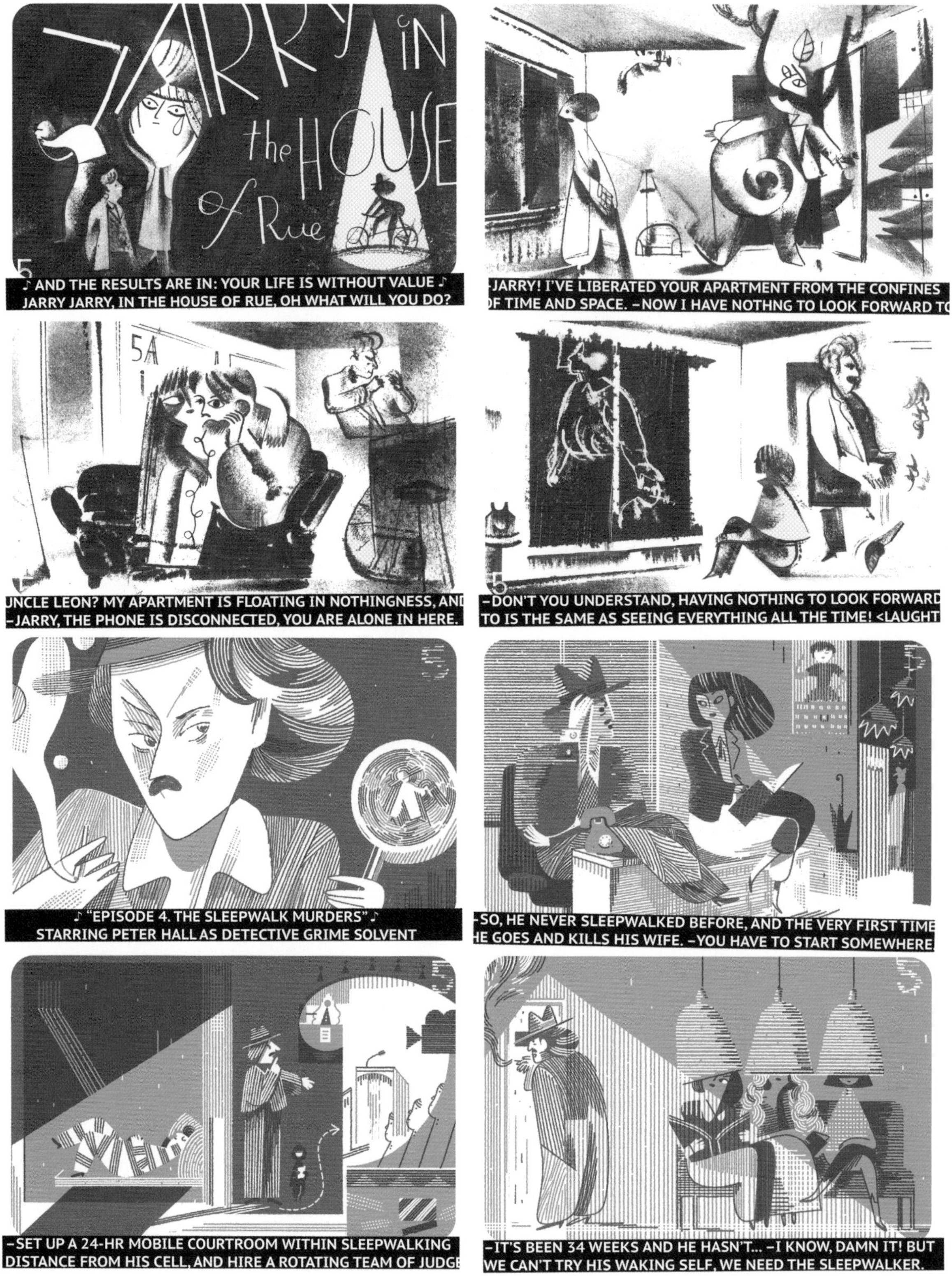
JARRY in the HOUSE of Rue
5
♪ AND THE RESULTS ARE IN: YOUR LIFE IS WITHOUT VALUE ♪
JARRY JARRY, IN THE HOUSE OF RUE, OH WHAT WILL YOU DO?
-JARRY! I'VE LIBERATED YOUR APARTMENT FROM THE CONFINES
OF TIME AND SPACE. –NOW I HAVE NOTHNG TO LOOK FORWARD TO
5A
UNCLE LEON? MY APARTMENT IS FLOATING IN NOTHINGNESS, AND
–JARRY, THE PHONE IS DISCONNECTED, YOU ARE ALONE IN HERE.
–DON'T YOU UNDERSTAND, HAVING NOTHING TO LOOK FORWARD
TO IS THE SAME AS SEEING EVERYTHING ALL THE TIME! <LAUGHT
♪ "EPISODE 4. THE SLEEPWALK MURDERS" ♪
STARRING PETER HALL AS DETECTIVE GRIME SOLVENT
-SO, HE NEVER SLEEPWALKED BEFORE, AND THE VERY FIRST TIME
HE GOES AND KILLS HIS WIFE. –YOU HAVE TO START SOMEWHERE.
–SET UP A 24-HR MOBILE COURTROOM WITHIN SLEEPWALKING
DISTANCE FROM HIS CELL, AND HIRE A ROTATING TEAM OF JUDGE
–IT'S BEEN 34 WEEKS AND HE HASN'T... –I KNOW, DAMN IT! BUT
WE CAN'T TRY HIS WAKING SELF, WE NEED THE SLEEPWALKER.

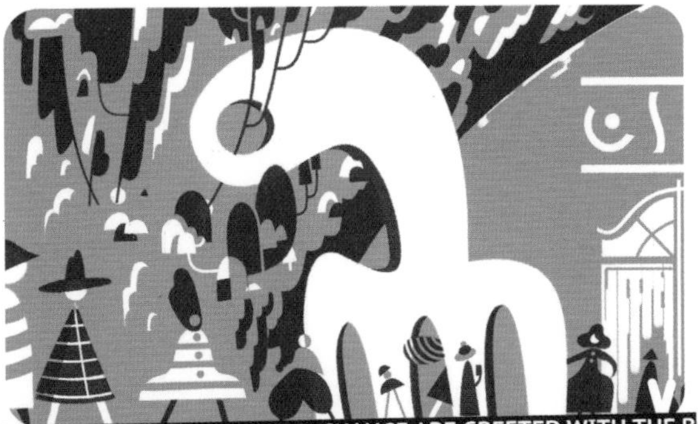

VISITORS TO THE OSLO ART EXCHANGE ARE GREETED WITH THE B
IDIOT FORK, A FORK WITH THREE TEETH INSTEAD OF FOUR, SIGNI

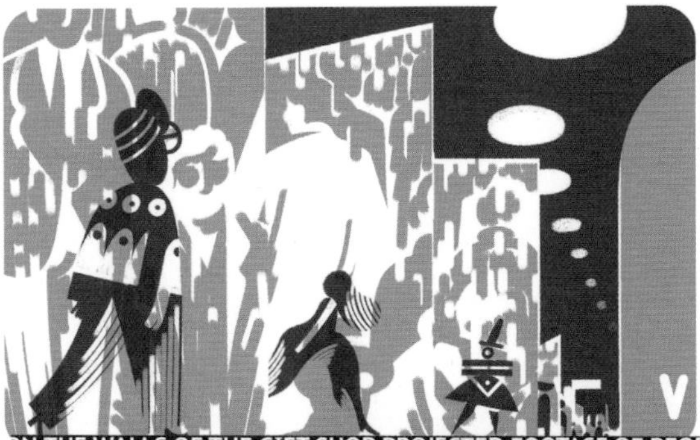

ON THE WALLS OF THE GIFT SHOP PROJECTED FOOTAGE OF PEOPL
WALKING AIMLESSLY IN DOCUMENTARIES—AN HOMAGE TO THE CO

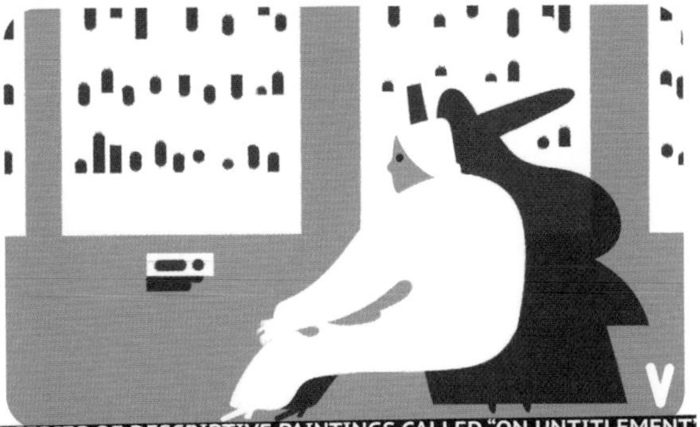

A SERIES OF DESCRIPTIVE PAINTINGS CALLED "ON UNTITLEMENT"
EACH OF THE UNTITLED CANVASES DESCRIBES ITSELF IN DETAIL T

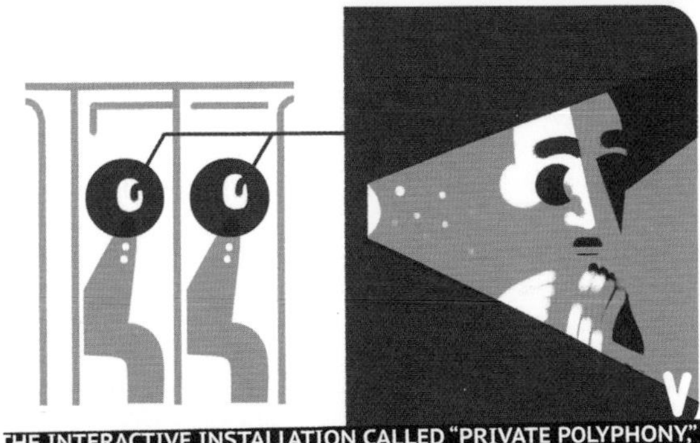

THE INTERACTIVE INSTALLATION CALLED "PRIVATE POLYPHONY," T
CONFESSION BOOTH ILLUMINATED ONLY BY THE PEEPHOLES THR

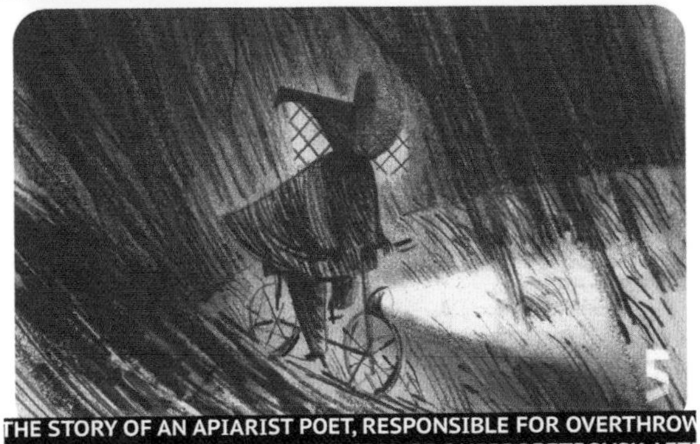

THE STORY OF AN APIARIST POET, RESPONSIBLE FOR OVERTHROW
SINGLEHANDEDLY THE CORRUPT CZAR OF DNEPROPETROVSK AFTE

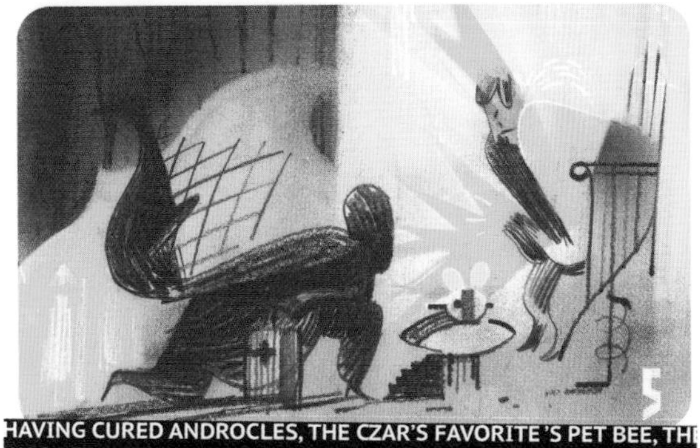

HAVING CURED ANDROCLES, THE CZAR'S FAVORITE 'S PET BEE, THE
WAS KNIGHTED ON THE SPOT AS THE ROYAL BEEKEPER, WITH ACC

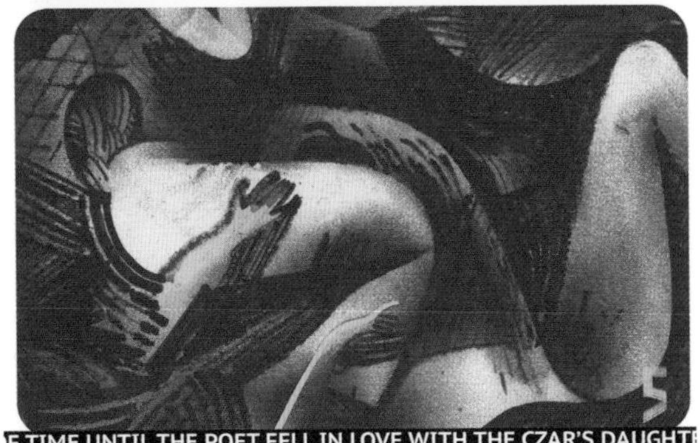

F TIME UNTIL THE POET FELL IN LOVE WITH THE CZAR'S DAUGHTE
WHOSE THIGHS WERE LACED WITH HONEY OF A DIFFERENT KIND.

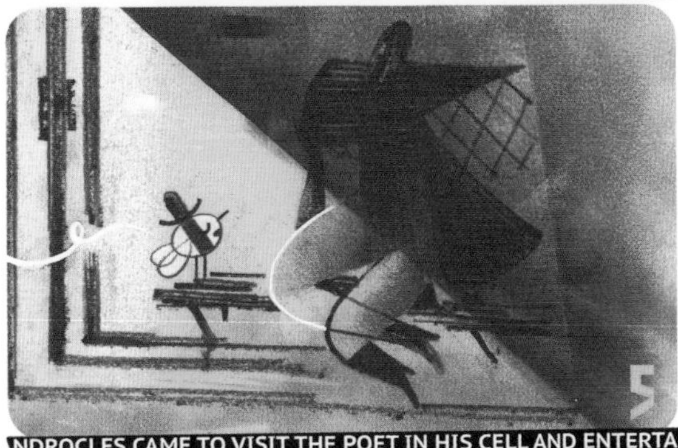

ANDROCLES CAME TO VISIT THE POET IN HIS CELL AND ENTERTAIN
HIM WITH A HYMENOPTRIC READING OF FOUCAULT'S DISCIPLINE

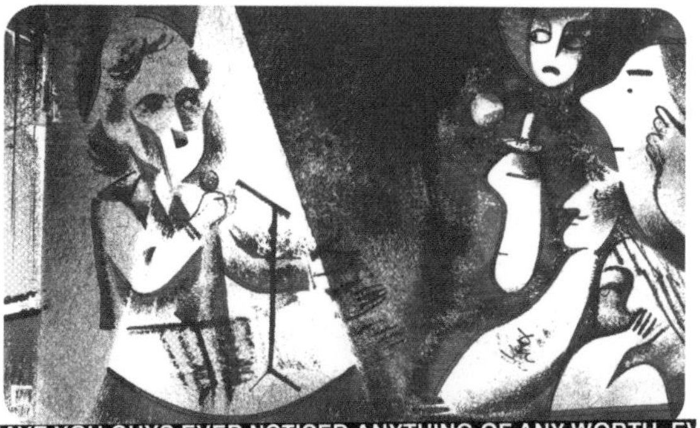

HAVE YOU GUYS EVER NOTICED ANYTHING OF ANY WORTH, EV
OUGH CROWD! COME ON, WE ARE ALONE IN THIS GODLESS UN

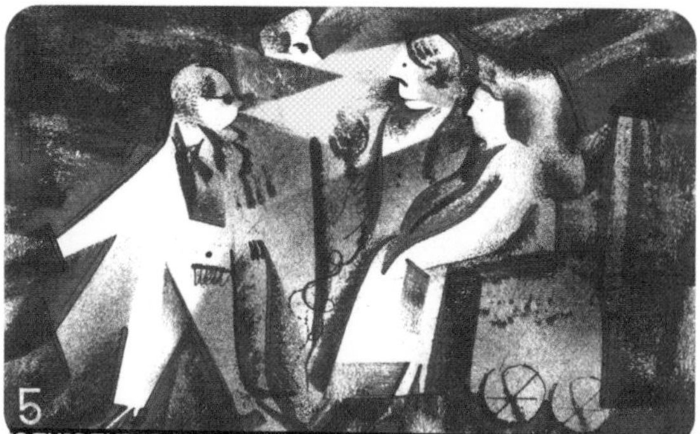

S THIS THING ON? <TAPS TWICE> THIS THING WAS NEVER ON. <T
TILL NORWARDS ON. AND ON. <TAP> AND ON. <TAP> AND ON. <TAP

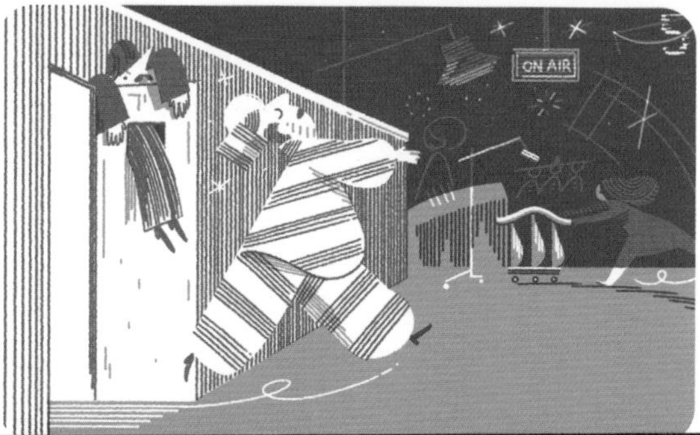
ON AIR

–QUICK, HE IS SLEEPWALKING! ASSEMBLE THE COURTROOM, SHH
WAKE THE STAFF AND PREPARE THE PROCEDURE! OH DO BE QUIET

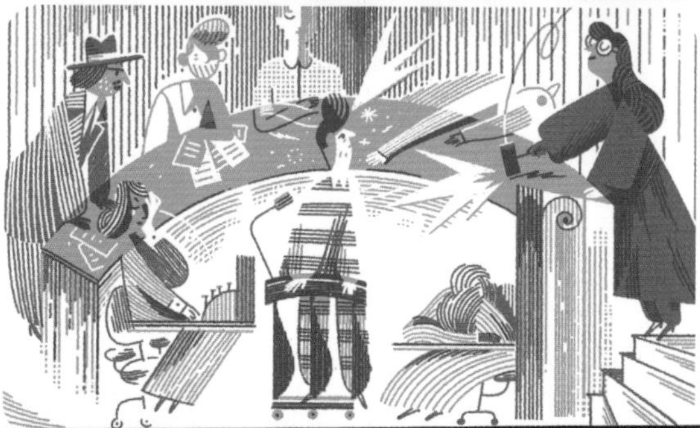

–SILENCE IN... <BANG> –HE WOKE UP! –FOR FUCK'S SAKE, WOMA
–I CAN'T JUDGE WITHOUT MY HAMMER! –BACK TO THE CELL WIT

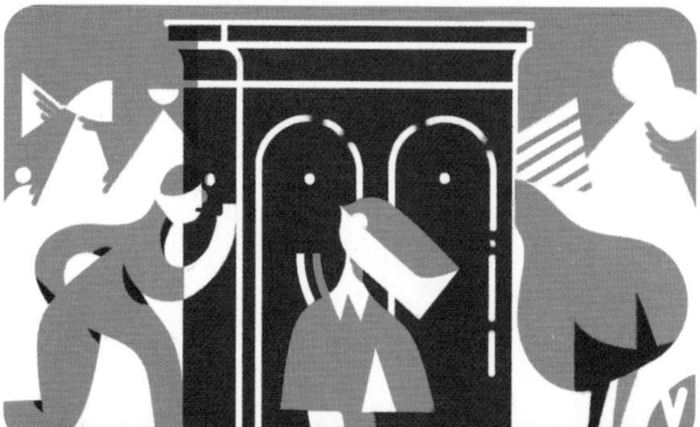

THE INSIDES OF THE CONFESSION BOOTH GROW DARKER AS MORE
PEOPLE ENGAGE WITH THE INSTALLATION, BLOCKING THE PEEPHO

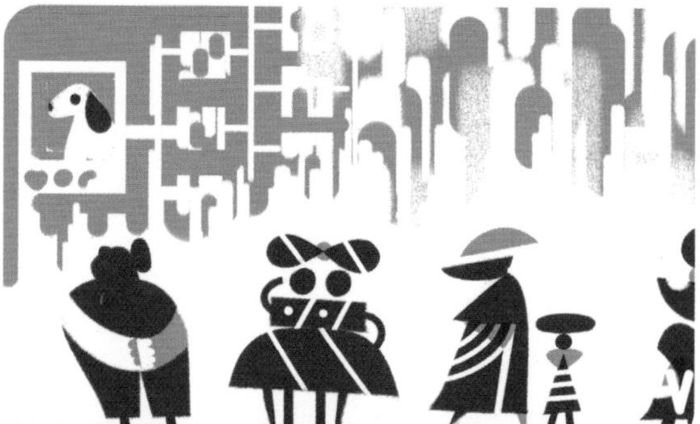

RESULTED IN THE PROJECT "LEAKED DOG," A COLLABORATION BET
HE OSLO EXCHANGE AND STUDIO 5: AN EXTENSIVE FLOWCHART D

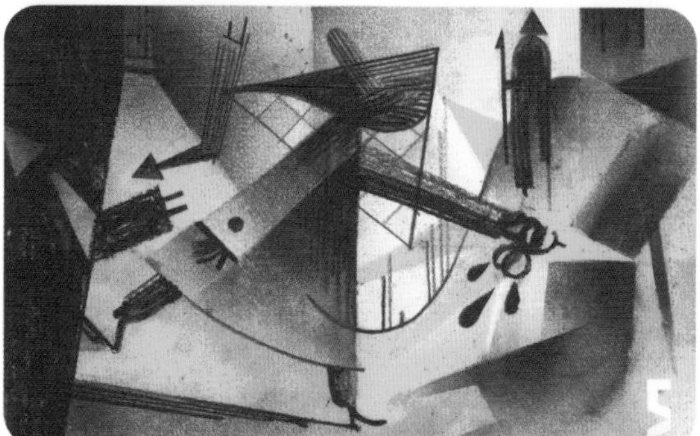

USED THE BEE TO PICK THE LOCK AND NEUTRALIZE THE GUARDS,
WITH THE BEE'S CONSENT--ANDROCLES TURNED TO BE AN ANARC

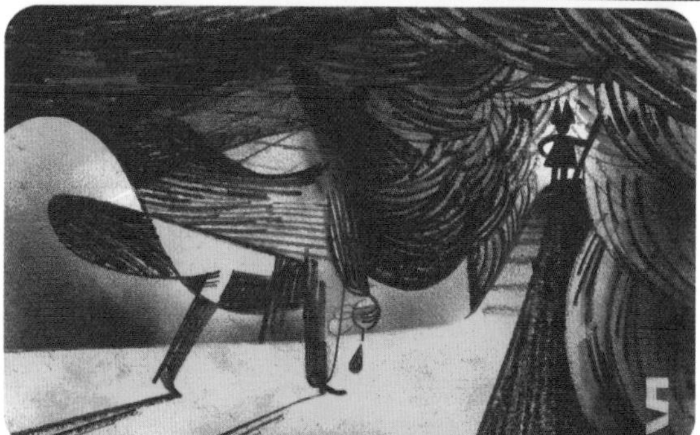

THREW THE CZAR OFF THE VERY LITERAL IVORY TOWER, AN ACT HE
THOUGHT NARRATIVELY CONTRIVED, BUT OTHERWISE QUITE APT.

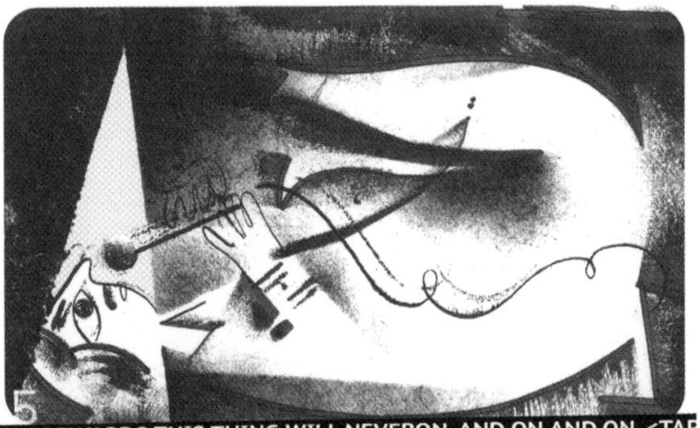

–NORWARDS THIS THING WILL NEVERON, AND ON AND ON. <TAP
TILL NORWARDS NO. <LOUD THUD> ♪ JARRY JARRY, WAIT AND SE

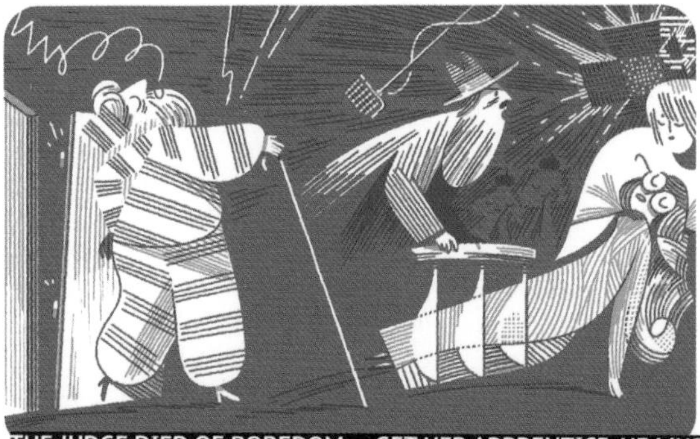

THE JUDGE DIED OF BOREDOM. –GET HER APPRENTICE, HE MUST
GRADUATED BY NOW, IT'S BEEN ELEVEN YEARS. –TWELVE! –SHUSH

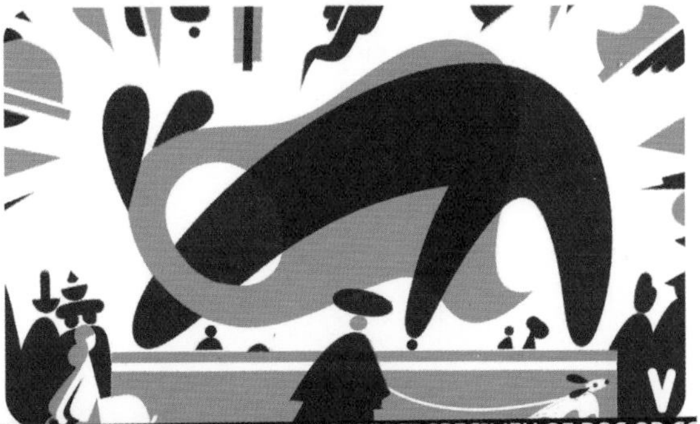

AN ATTEMPT TO PRODUCE THE PERFECT SPECIMEN OF DOG OR GO
IN AT LEAST TWELVE YEARS TO COME. THIS CONCLUDES OUR TOUR

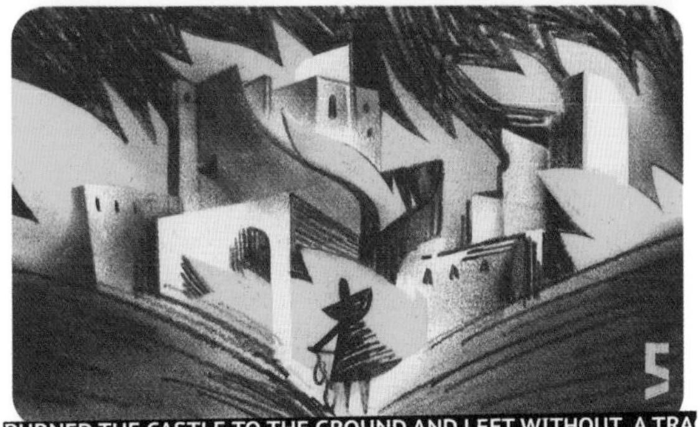

BURNED THE CASTLE TO THE GROUND AND LEFT WITHOUT A TRA
A PERFECT BLANK, UNSULLIED BY SEX OR POETRY OR BEEKEEPING

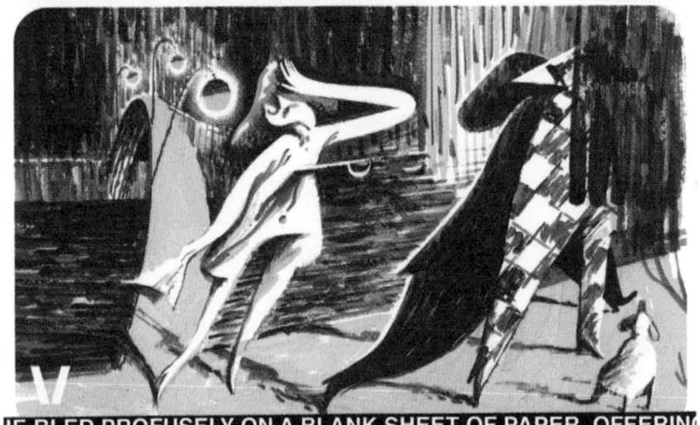

HE BLED PROFUSELY ON A BLANK SHEET OF PAPER, OFFERING
TO ANY PASSERBY, UNTIL HE DIED UNDER THE ELMS OF RUE S

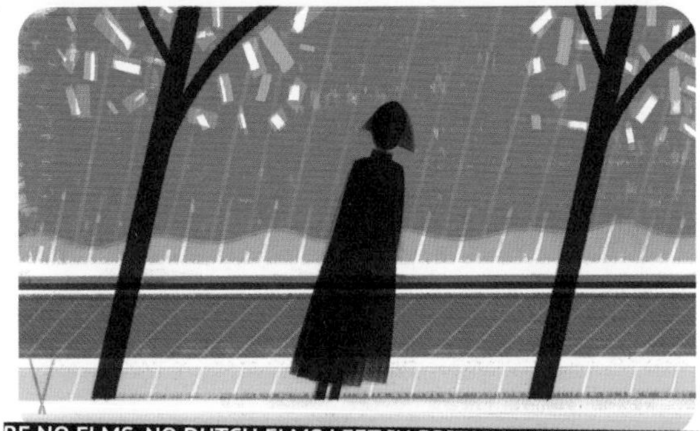

RE NO ELMS, NO DUTCH ELMS LEFT IN BRITAIN, ACCORDING TO TH
RINGS OF OF SATURN, AND FEWER STILL ELM SUBSTITUES, ONCE F

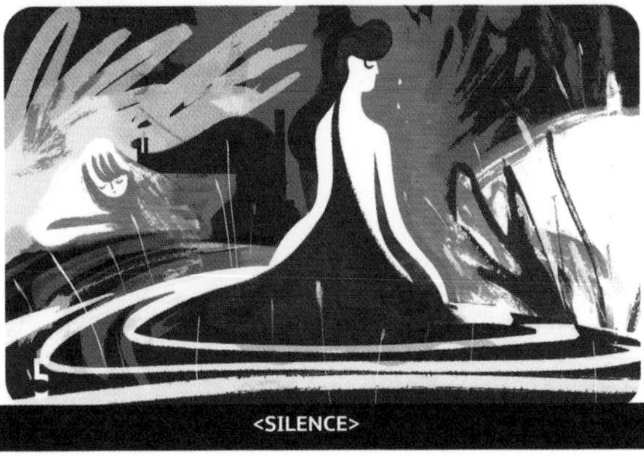

<SILENCE>

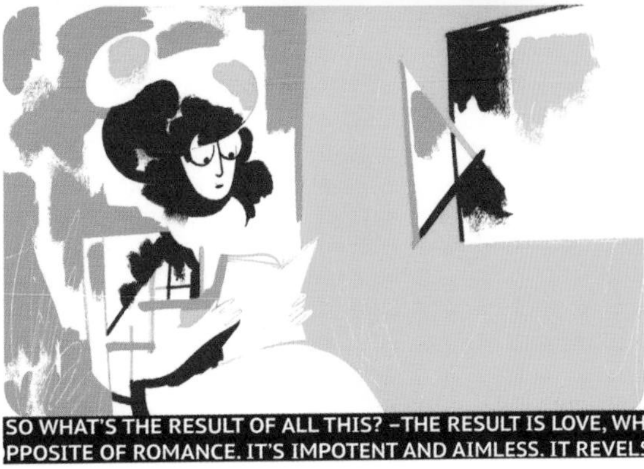

SO WHAT'S THE RESULT OF ALL THIS? –THE RESULT IS LOVE, WHIC
PPOSITE OF ROMANCE. IT'S IMPOTENT AND AIMLESS. IT REVELS I

ACT 12
The Interview

CAST
T. B.
M. Fallotin

SCENE
Studio 5, film room
Mild Street
"Vanishing Act"

TIME
23:30-23:50

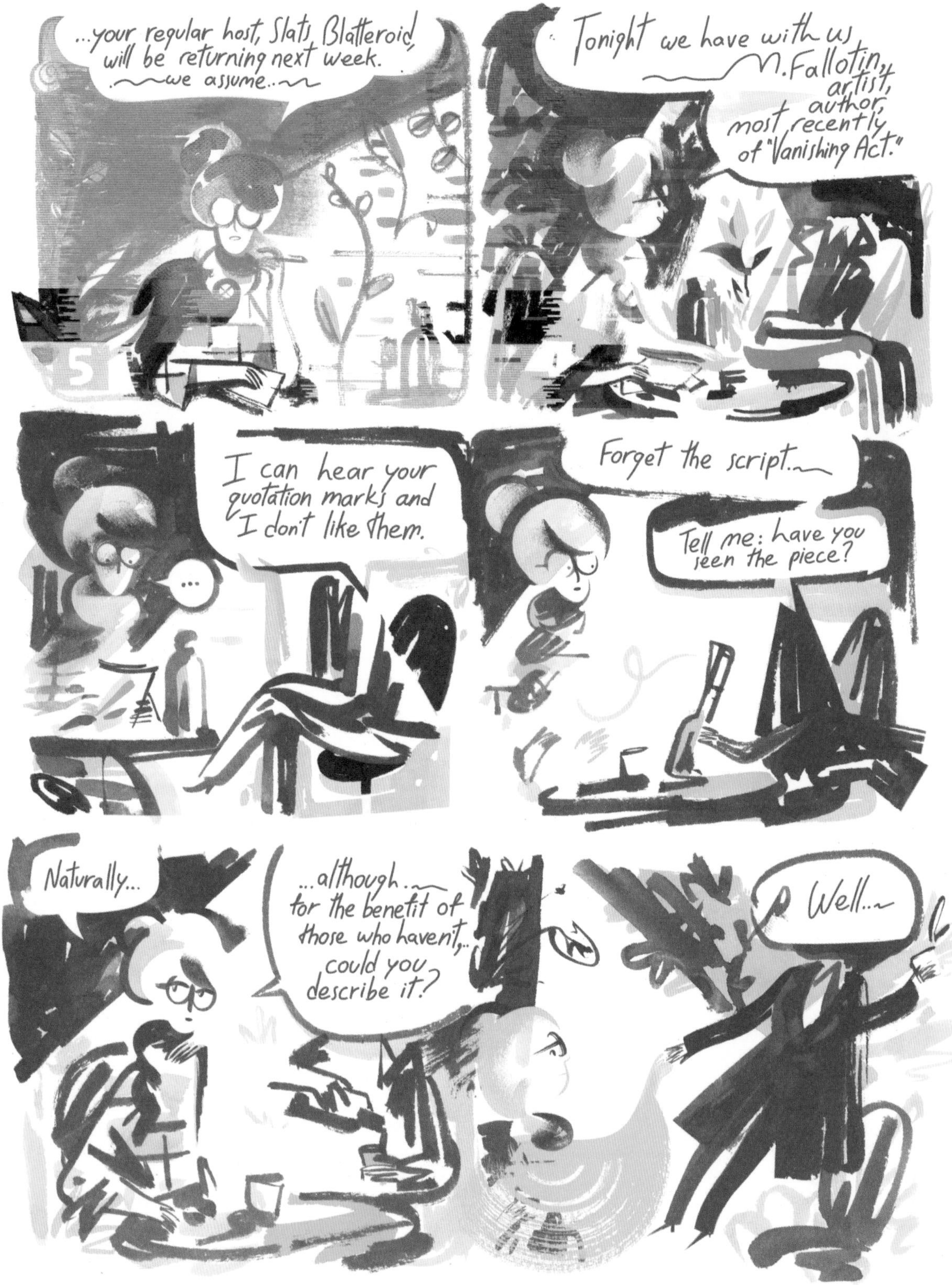
...your regular host, Slats Blatteroid, will be returning next week.
...we assume...
Tonight we have with us M. Fallotin, artist, author, most recently of "Vanishing Act."
...
I can hear your quotation marks and I don't like them.
Forget the script...
Tell me: have you seen the piece?
Naturally...
...although... for the benefit of those who haven't... could you describe it?
Well...

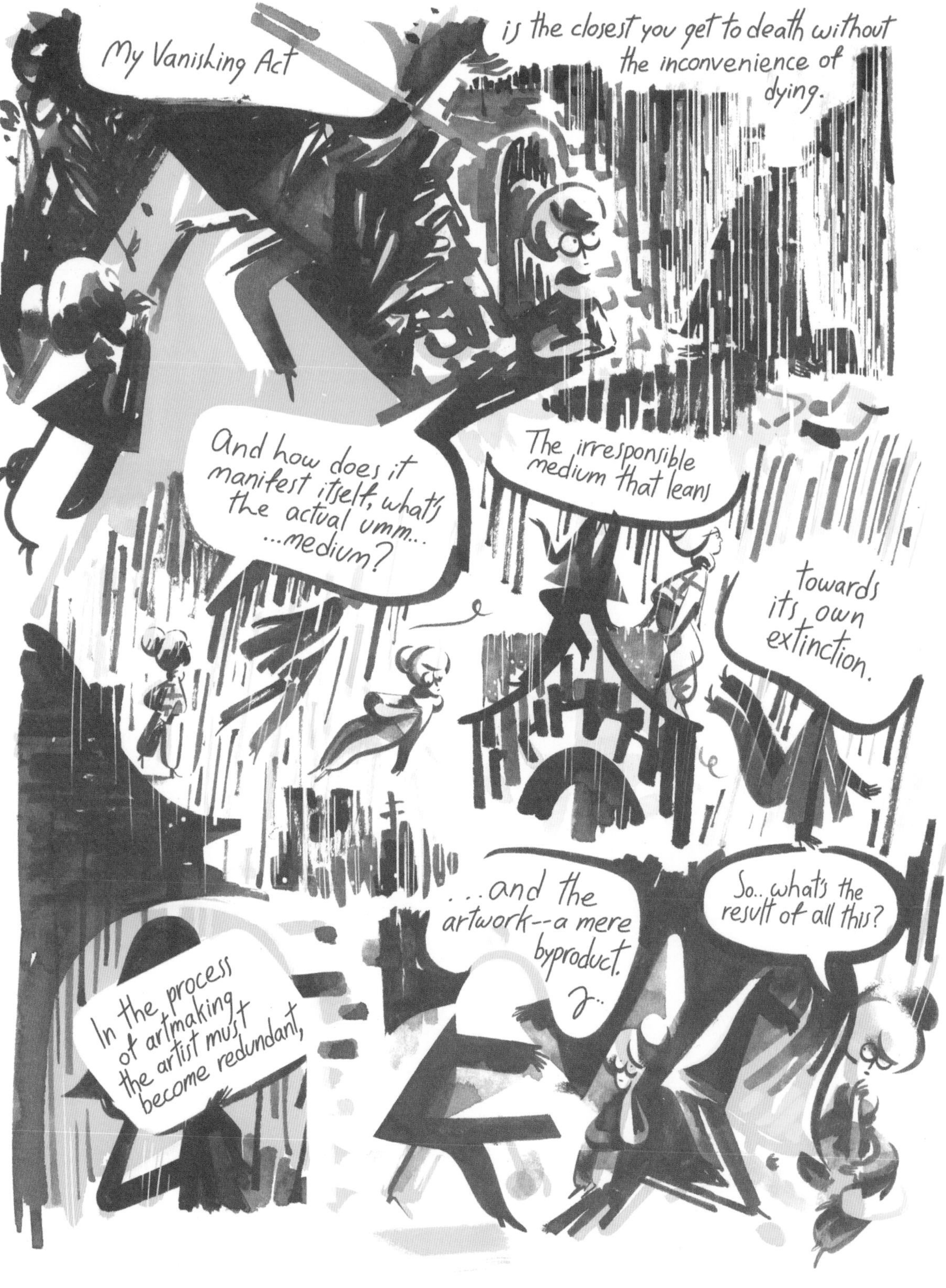

My Vanishing Act
is the closest you get to death without the inconvenience of dying.
And how does it manifest itself, what's the actual umm... ...medium?
The irresponsible medium that leans
towards its own extinction.
In the process of artmaking the artist must become redundant,
...and the artwork--a mere byproduct.
So... what's the result of all this?

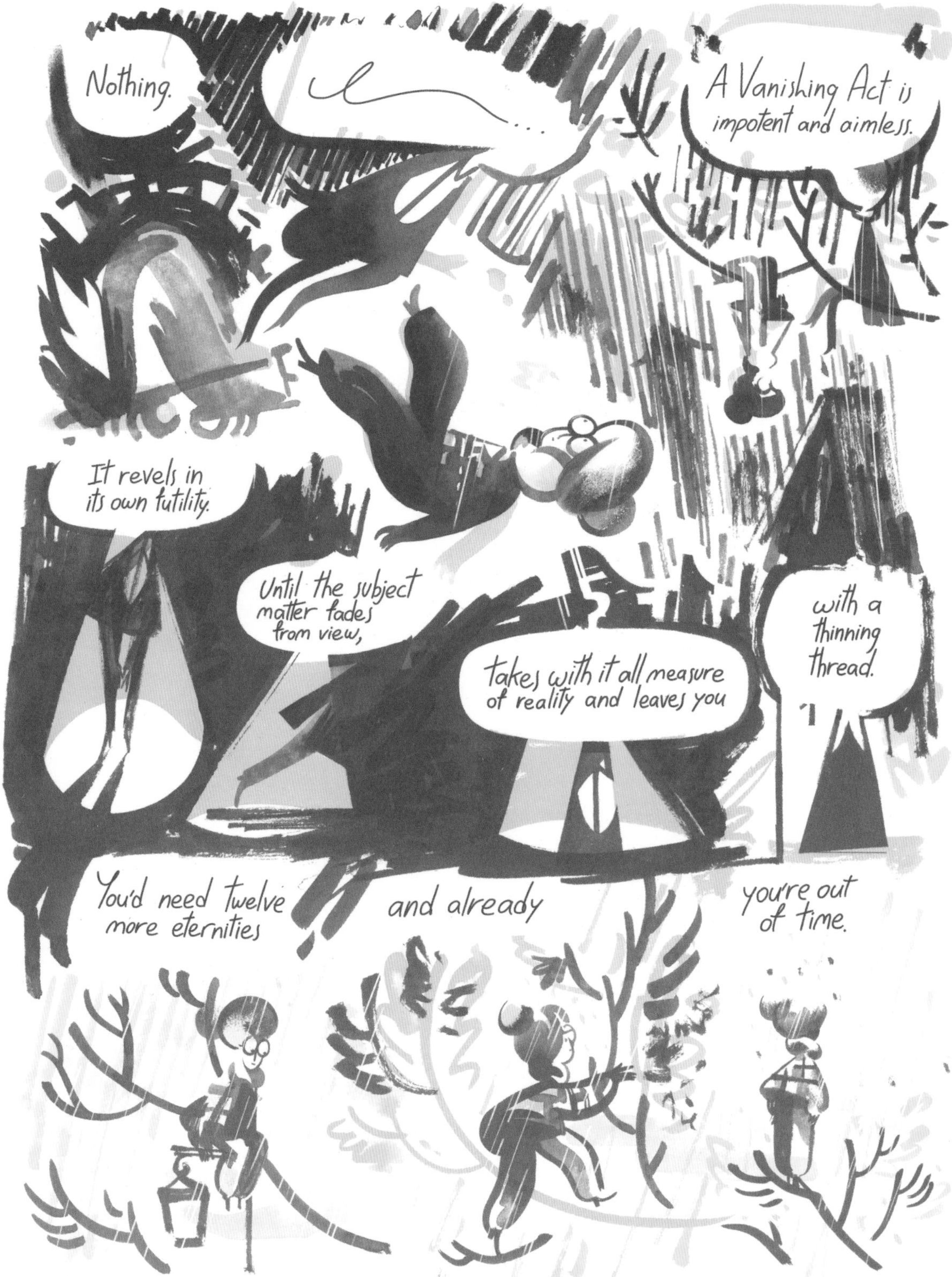
Nothing.
A Vanishing Act is impotent and aimless.
It revels in its own futility.
Until the subject matter fades from view,
takes with it all measure of reality and leaves you
with a thinning thread.
You'd need twelve more eternities
and already
you're out of time.

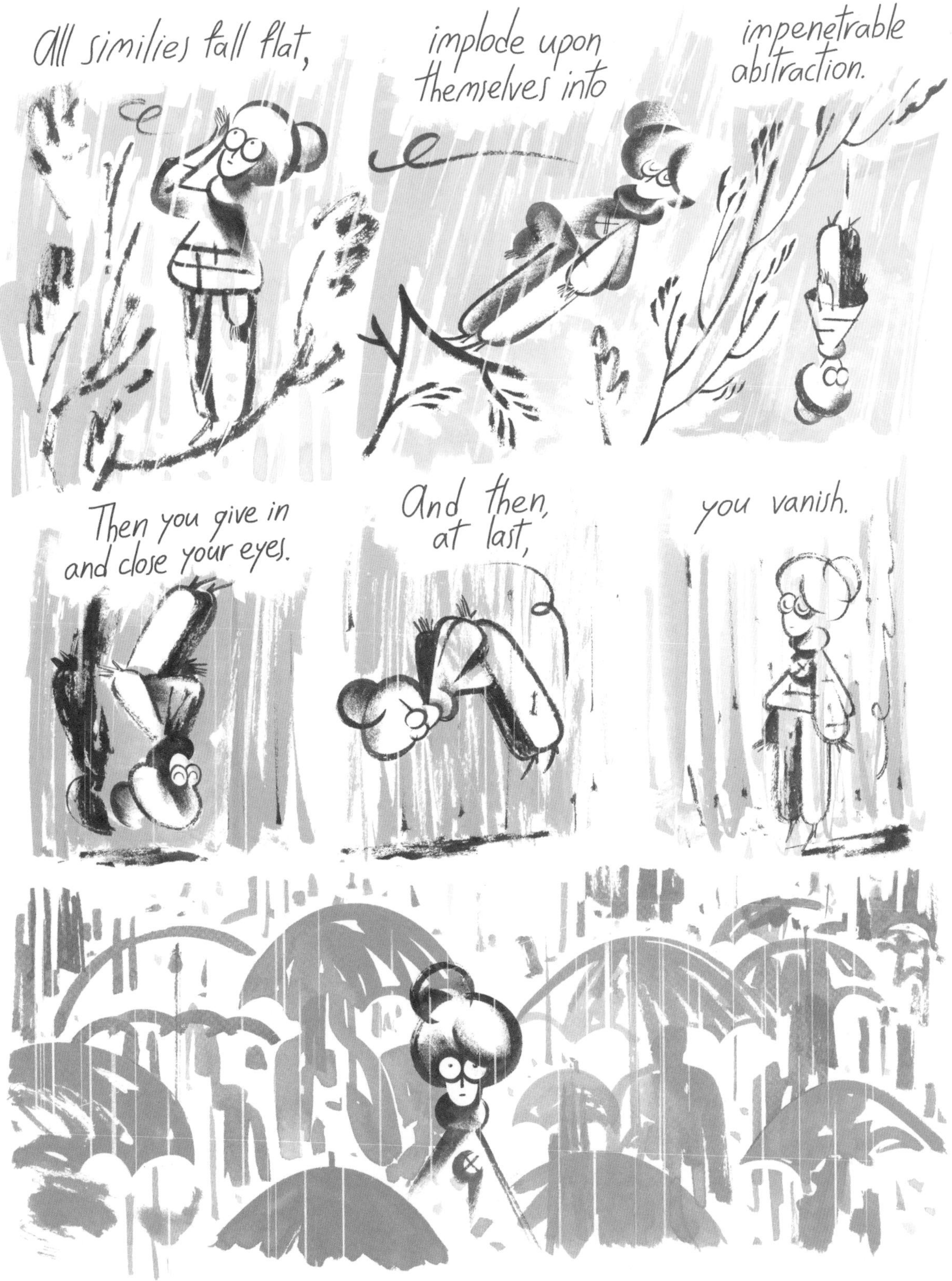
All similies fall flat,
implode upon themselves into
impenetrable abstraction.
Then you give in and close your eyes.
And then, at last,
you vanish.

ACT 13
The Party

CAST
Sybil Same

SCENE
Sybil Same's apartment

TIME
23:40-XX:XX

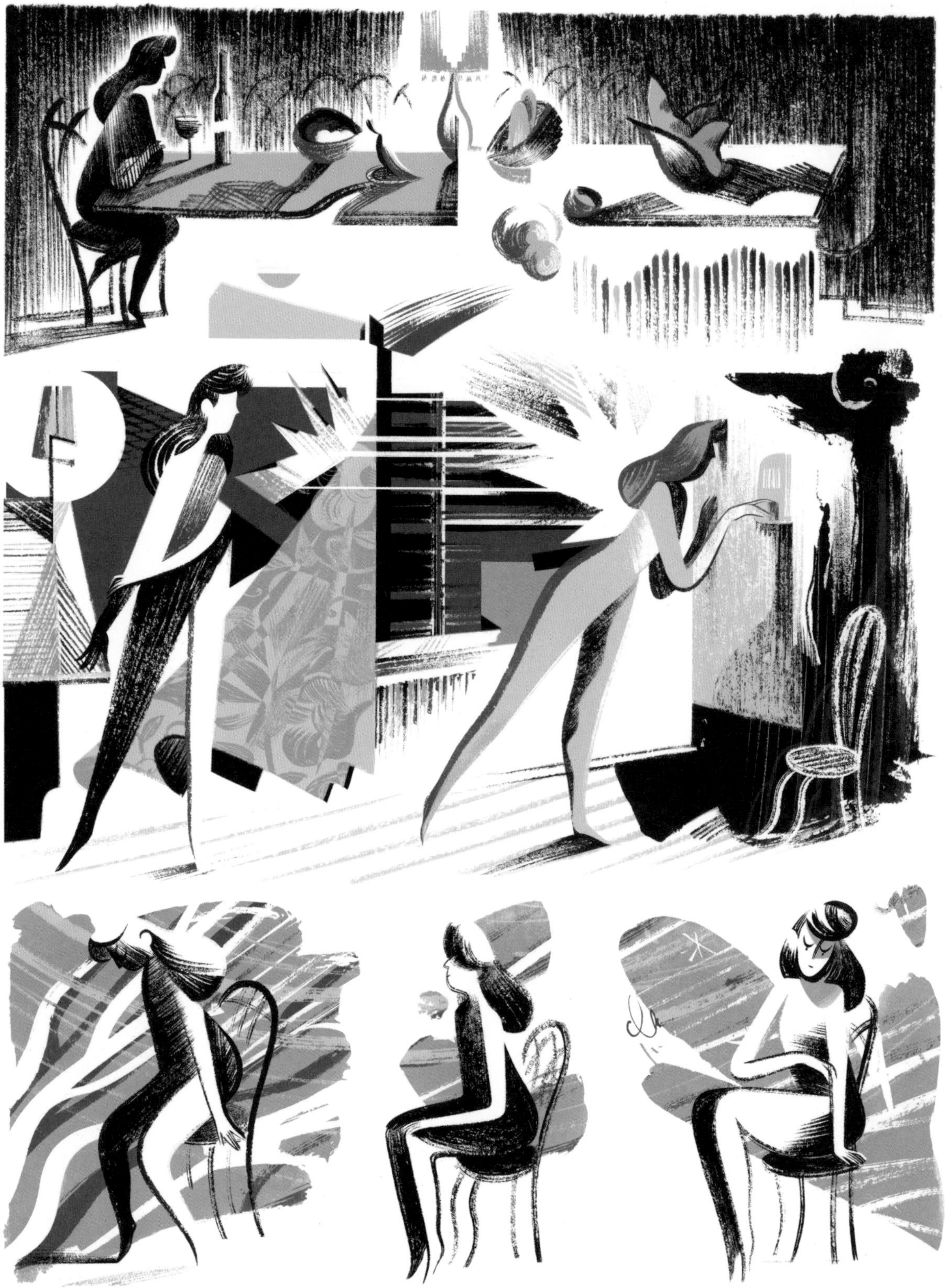

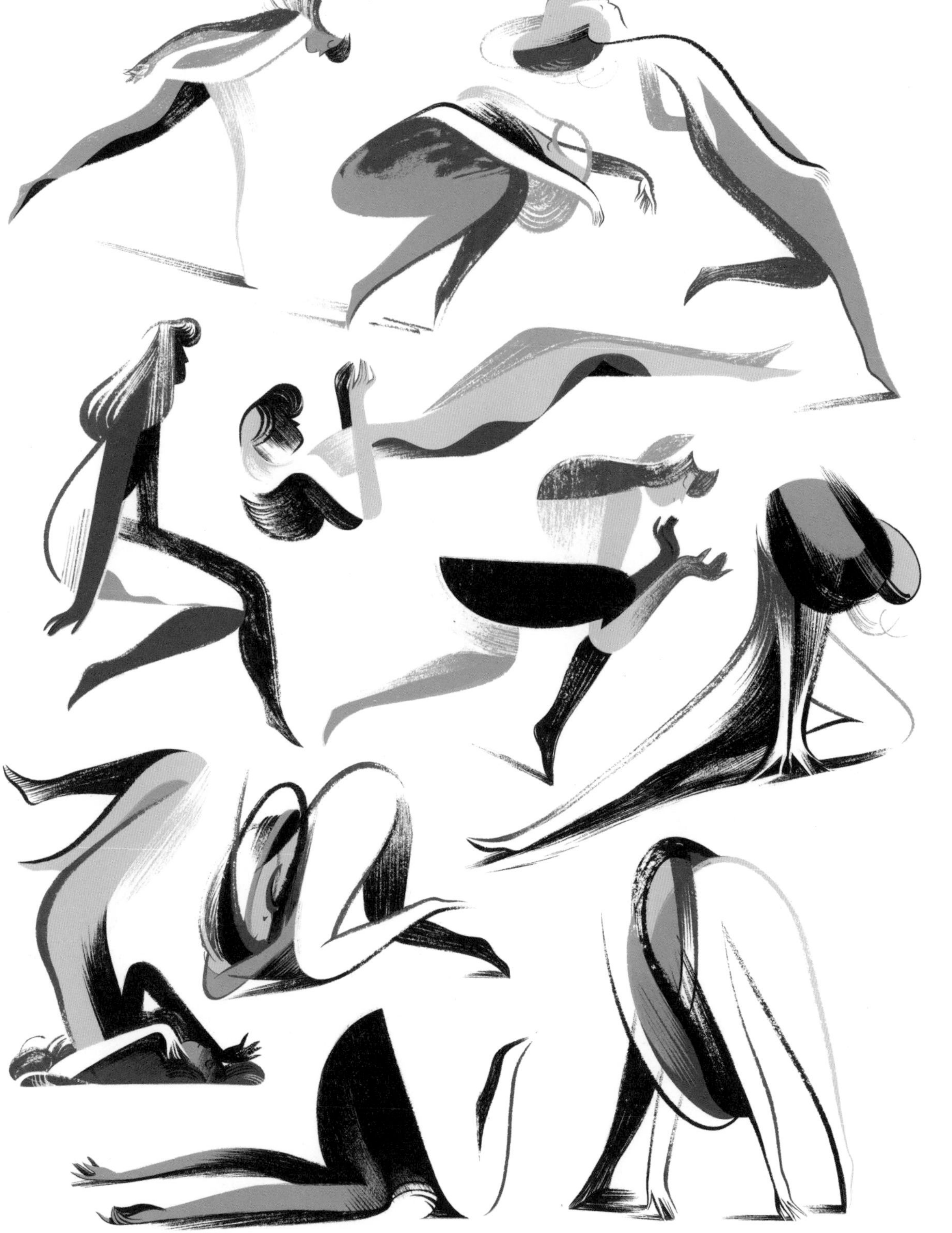

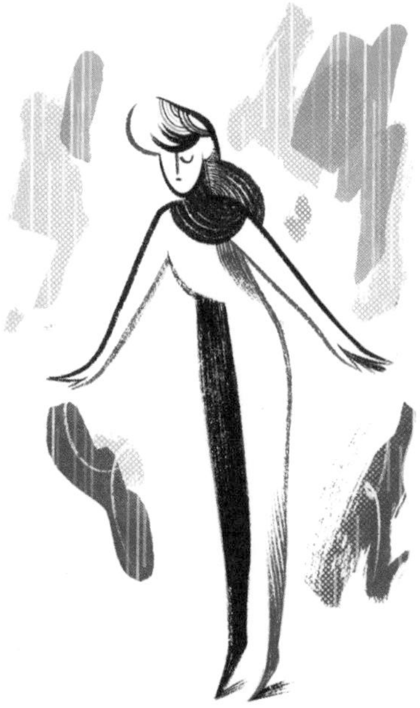
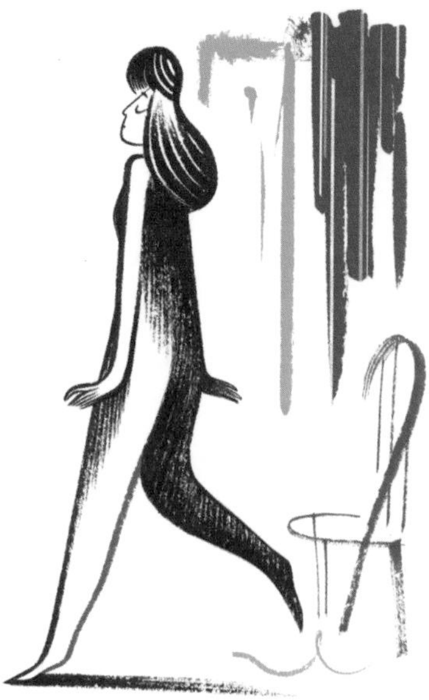
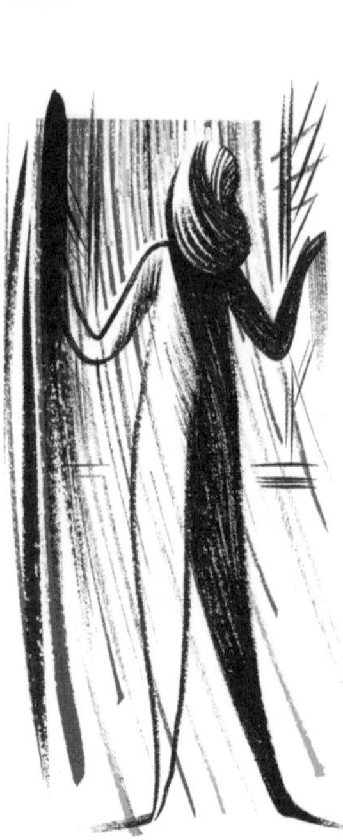
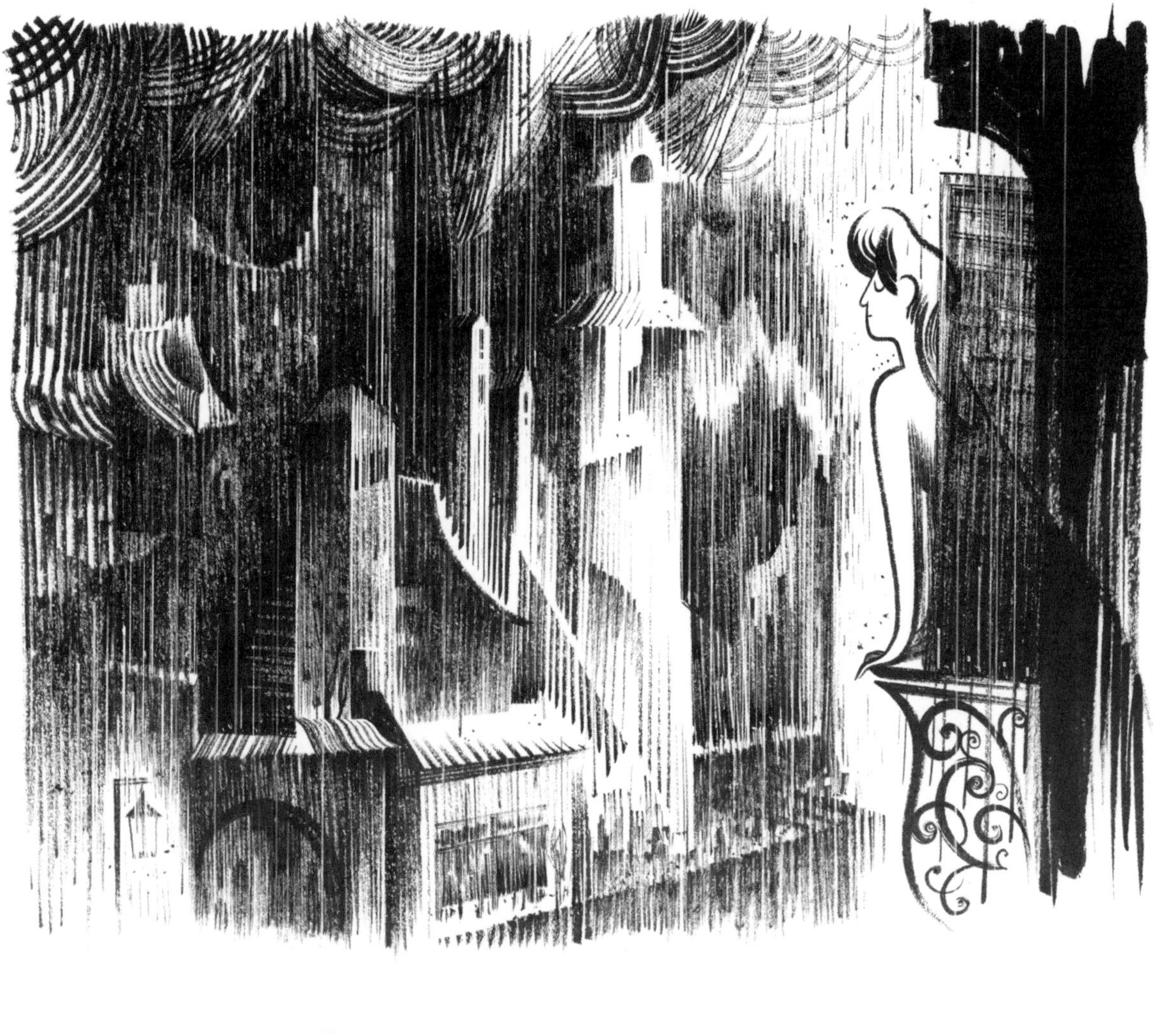

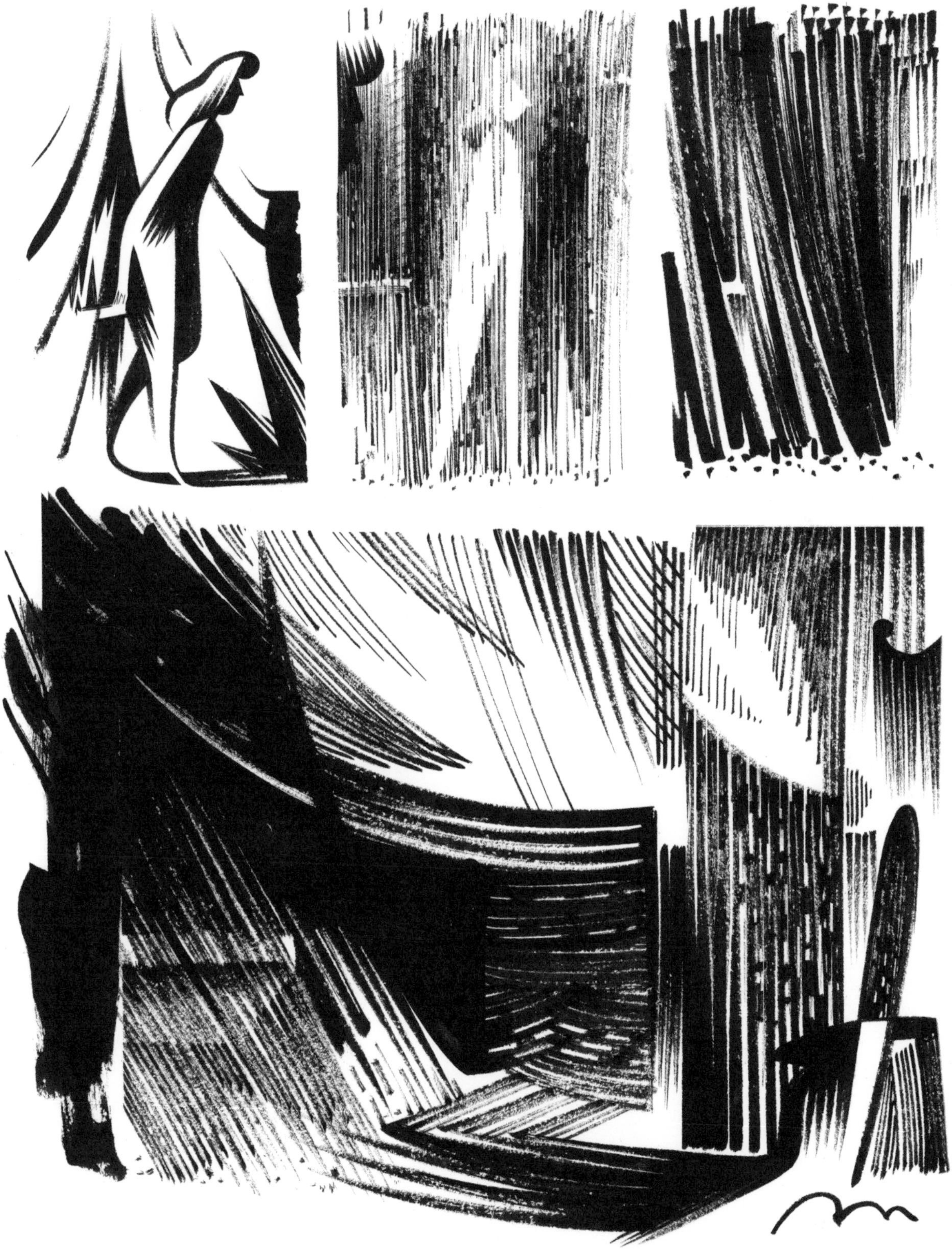

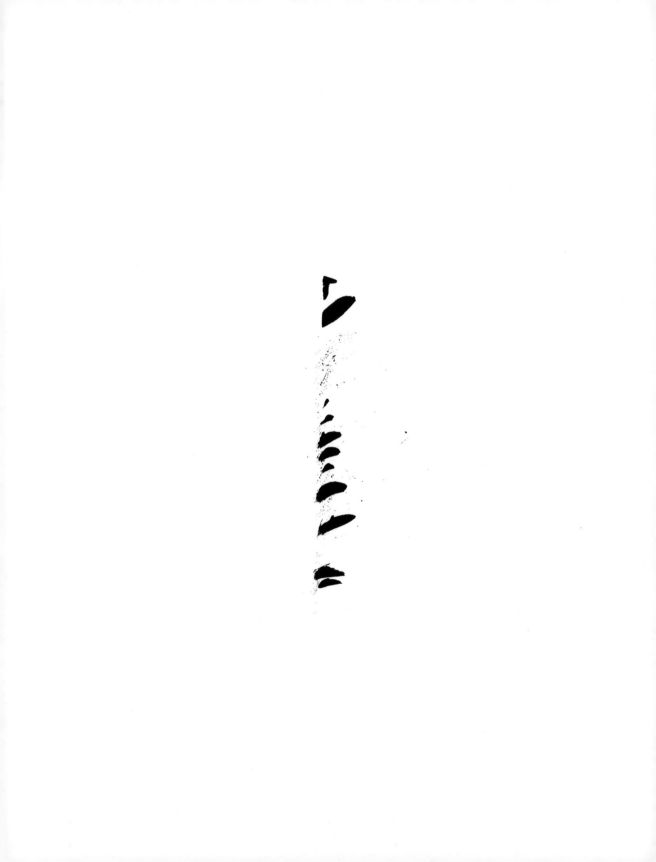

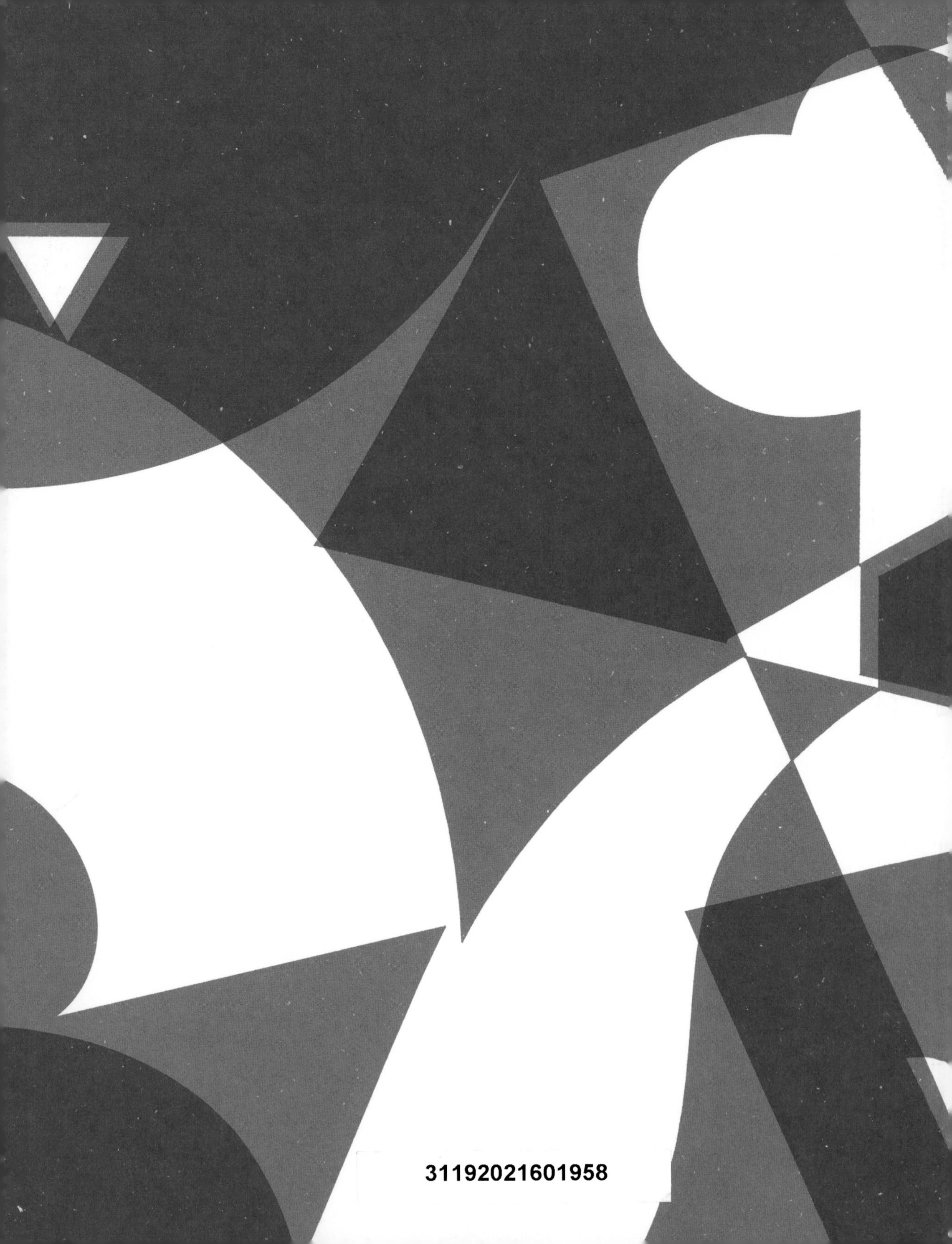